A CANDLELIGHT INTRIGUE

CANDLELIGHT INTRIGUES

RUTHANA

MARGARET NETTLES OGAN

A CANDLELIGHT INTRIGUE

Published by
Dell Publishing Co., Inc.
1 Dag Hammarskjold Plaza
New York, New York 10017

Dell ® TM 681510, Dell Publishing Co., Inc.

ISBN: 0-440-18208-5

Printed in the United States of America
First printing—April 1980

To Faye and Lee

CHAPTER 1

With Christmas only two days away, cold rain drenched New York; North Atlantic winter weather promised sleet or snow. The small alarm clock on the table beside her bed awakened Ruthana Franklin from a troubled sleep. For a moment she couldn't remember why she'd set the alarm.

When she'd tumbled into bed the night before, Ruthana had been exhausted from fending off the unwelcome advances of Alexander Farnsworth III. She remembered that well enough!

He'd completely spoiled what could have been a pleasant evening.

"Damn the man!" Ruthana brushed a honey-blonde strand of hair away from her high fore-head. "If I never see *him* again it will be too soon!"

Living at home in Philadelphia, Ruthana had dated Alex Farnsworth a few times last year when he was in town for the holiday season. She remembered him as pleasant company, but since then he'd been traveling abroad. They'd exchanged a few friendly letters, and he'd called her from Athens just to say hello. So Ruthana was pleased when he called yesterday morning to invite her for a night at the theater. She hadn't been able to get herself a ticket, at a price she could afford, for the Broadway hit *Holiday for Two*.

For the past year Ruthana had earned her living by working as a fashion model in New York. It came as a surprise, when she saw Alex again, to realize how dull a person the man really was. His jet-set gossip was a bore, and Ruthana couldn't have cared less when he re-counted his polo triumphs in Madrid. Who was dating whose wife on the French Riviera didn't impress Ruthana. But she'd enjoyed the play and looked forward to their late supper at the Four Winds.

The food was good, and momentarily Alex forgot to talk about himself, asking questions about her career as a model. But asking him up to her small Fifty-ninth Street apartment for a nightcap was a mistake, and one she didn't intend to make again with any man.

"Ruthana, I want to know you better," Alex had said, taking her in his arms.

It took a minute for Ruthana to realize how much better Alex intended to know her. That embrace rapidly degenerated into a struggle. Unable to match Alex's strength, as a last resort Ruthana drove a knee into his groin. The ripped dress on a hanger in her closet was mute testimony to the fierceness of the struggle with Alex Farnsworth.

Suddenly Ruthana remembered why she'd set her alarm for eight o'clock and damned Alex again for nearly making her forget she had an appointment with Hugh Laidman. She was due at his West Twenty-third Street photographic studio at ten.

Ruthana scampered from her bed to the bath-

room, shedding her nightgown on the way. A
long shower eased the muscles strained during
her struggle with Alex and washed away the
feeling she had that his hands had left their
print on her body. Ruthana smiled when she
remembered the shocked expression on his face
when she had to use her knee to cool his ardor.

Ruthana's mother considered Alexander
Farnsworth III the most eligible bachelor in
Mainline Philadelphia, and with Alex's inherited
wealth, Mother was probably right, Ruthana
thought. But who needs a man with only one
thing, aside from polo ponies, on his mind?
Ruthana decided she definitely didn't.

She wiped memories of last night out of her
conscious mind because her session with Hugh
today would be the most important of her
modeling career. Other models would gladly
pay, and some had offered to do so, just to be
photographed by Hugh Laidman, the most
prestigious high-fashion photographer in New
York.

Ruthana was honored that Hugh had selected
her and Penny Andrews to pose in Madame
Yvonne's resort and swimwear collection. Her
modeling future was assured if she could please

Hugh Laidman. Today he planned to make test shots of her and Penny before they flew down to the Caribbean island of Saba in the Netherlands Antilles. They would leave for Saba on Christmas Day, for three weeks of working on location. But today she would have to be at her sparkling best because it wasn't too late for Hugh to select another model.

During the last year Ruthana had proved she had modeling ability and could stand the strain of long hours under hot lights. Her mother thought Ruthana was dabbling at a modeling career and would soon think better of it. But the girl prided herself on being every inch a professional.

While toweling down, Ruthana studied her body in the full-length mirror and was delighted to discover that in his mauling Alex hadn't bruised her anywhere. She had an athletic body that, at the same time, was entirely feminine. Her legs were tapered and slim, her stomach flat, her breasts not too large. Her gray-green eyes were clear, and a quick brushing was all her shoulder-length blonde hair needed. It was naturally wavy, a real boon to Ruthana. She had to be careful with her money and appreciated the fact that she seldom had to patronize a beauty parlor.

An art director had once told Ruthana that she was virginally sensuous.

Making coffee and squeezing orange juice in the kitchenette, Ruthana remembered what a surprise Hugh Laidman had been. She'd learned that almost all the good photographers in New York were ugly men and careless of their appearance. Thirty top-fashion models had crowded Madame Yvonne's salon the other afternoon. Until he'd finally selected Penny Andrews and her, Ruthana didn't realize the tall man in tweeds, who smoked a pipe, was Hugh Laidman. With Laidman's strong but classical features, Ruthana had mistaken him for a male model! The Man of Distinction type.

From other models who'd worked for him, Ruthana knew Hugh was a demanding perfectionist and had reduced more than one girl to tears. She'd also learned from the other girls that he was immune to their feminine charm.

"The man is either gay or a monk," she'd heard one girl tell another. "*Venus de Milo* in the flesh wouldn't rate a pass from the great Hugh Laidman!"

Hugh had put it very simply to Ruthana. "I want to work with you and Penny Andrews, unless you have other plans. I wouldn't want to ruin your holidays."

"I can't think of a better way to spend my Christmas holidays than a trip to the Caribbean," Ruthana said, with a smile.

"Good. We have a deal, then." Hugh returned her smile. "Come to my studio the day after tomorrow at ten o'clock, and we'll make some test shots."

It was Hugh's smile that did it. The way it lighted his face stirred a dangerous longing in Ruthana, and a tightness in her throat warned the girl she would have to be careful. Working closely with all types of men during the past year, Ruthana had studiously avoided any emotional involvements. She knew other girls at the agency nicknamed her the Ice Maiden.

I'll have to watch myself very closely with Hugh Laidman, Ruthana thought, buttering her toast.

His quick smile had tapped a wellspring of emotion within Ruthana that no other man had ever reached. She felt vulnerable and a little afraid.

13

* *. *

Otto, the doorman of her apartment building, greeted Ruthana with a wide smile. "A very good morning to you, Miss Franklin," he said with the trace of a German accent. "You've got the hatbox I see. On a day as bad as this one you should model rubbers and raincoats."

Otto had treated Ruthana as if she were his daughter from the first day she'd moved into the building.

Ruthana laughed. "I wish I were, Otto, but it's swimwear. Can you imagine?"

"You'll catch cold, Miss Franklin. What kind of dunderhead would have you put on a swimsuit in this kind of weather? You should stay in bed on a day as bad as this."

"I wish that I could, Otto, but the rent has a way of coming due," Ruthana said. "Can you get me a cab? I don't want to show up for this appointment looking like a drowned rabbit."

Otto reached for his rain cape. "Anything for you, Miss Franklin. I'll have to swim over to Fifth. Get over there by the heater and warm yourself."

Within a few minutes Otto was back with a cab, and Ruthana knew he'd jotted down the driver's license number and memorized his face. Before Ruthana reached her destination, Otto would have called the taxi dispatcher.

"You're a model, ain't you?" The driver glanced at the hatbox on the seat beside Ruthana. He was a grizzled, elderly man, in need of a shave. "I got a lot of respect for you girls. Modeling is as hard work as driving a hack, ain't it?"

"We don't have to contend with muggers and holdup men," Ruthana said. "But we do work hard."

The driver groaned. "Animals! That's what New York and Brooklyn breed these days. Fun City!" He snorted. "That John Lindsay." He wagged his head. "Animals we got. Did you ever look at Times Square lately? Sex! How did that get out of the bedroom?"

Ruthana laughed. "Don't ask me."

"You ain't a New Yorker. I've got an ear for accents. Where are you from?"

"Philadelphia."

"A cemetery with street lights!" The driver grinned back at her. "No offense, pretty lady. I ain't ever been west of the Hudson. New York is my town. How can you beat it? All the action is here. Do you model styles?"

"I have," Ruthana said. Since coming to New York, Ruthana had discovered she had easy rapport with cab drivers, doormen, children, and the elderly. "Do you know anyone on Seventh Avenue?"

"My son, Max, works for Gottleib. Gottleib Suits and Coats. Do you know them?"

"Very well. They're a good house."

"You want something wholesale, I'll give you Max's card. Max is going to be a doctor. He goes to NYU nights, hustles garments for Gottleib days."

"You have an ambitious son," Ruthana said.

"That's our Max," the driver said with pride. "Me and Sarah only got the one kid." He was weaving his cab down Fifth Avenue, through the Christmas rush. "You should have seen his Bar Mitzvah. The whole neighborhood turned out. We got a Polish rabbi, but he's smart. I bet your folks worry about you, up here in Sin City."

"My mother does. My father died when I was a child."

"Hey, too bad. My old man is dead, and the old lady, too, since September. I was brought up in the South Bronx. It's Fort Apache now, but a good family neighborhood when I was a kid. Everybody knew everybody else." Sol Lebberman swung the cab in toward the curb on West Twenty-third and swept down the flag. "Here we are, pretty lady."

"Thank you, Mr. Lebberman." She'd learned his name from the license in a frame below the meter. "You have yourself a good day."

Sol regarded the generous tip in the palm of his hand. "You sure ain't a New Yorker," he said. "You have a good day, too."

Ruthana faced one of a row of remodeled loft buildings. She glanced at her digital watch, another gift from her mother, this time on her birthday, February 1. It was only quarter to ten.

Punctuality had become a fetish with Ruthana during the past year. She'd learned that time is money in the high-pressure world of fashion photography and advertising. Being five minutes late for an appointment could draw disapproving glances from highly paid photographers and account executives.

There was no elevator. Swinging her black hatbox, Ruthana climbed the stairs to the third floor and found herself facing a polished, golden oak door, with a simple brass plate that said: HUGH LAIDMAN, PHOTOS.

Opening the door, Ruthana found herself in a small carpeted anteroom, facing a receptionist's desk, but no one was behind it. Because she'd heard a discreet buzzer inside the studio apartment when she opened the door, Ruthana waited.

Wearing tan whipcord slacks and a dark brown sweater-shirt, open at the throat, Hugh Laidman stepped into the small anteroom with a coffee mug in his hand. His pipe and a tobacco pouch were in the pocket of his shirt.

"You're ahead of time, Franklin." That smile again! "My girl called in sick this morning, and so did Penny Andrews."

"I'm sorry. Will you need me?" Ruthana asked.

"I surely do." Hugh brushed the lock of reddish-brown hair that had fallen across his broad forehead. "Penny will model the frocks and beach caps. I want you for the swimwear. Madame Yvonne wants to see you in her bikinis. I do, too," Hugh admitted. "Come on, let's get a cup of coffee in you first. Some kind

18

of a New York day, isn't it I hope you took a cab."

"I did, and with a talkative driver," Ruthana said. "Sol Lebberman."

Hugh laughed. "I hacked for a few months when I first came to New York from the sticks."

Hugh stood aside for Ruthana to enter his studio apartment. She found herself in a high-ceilinged, large room that stretched from the front of the building to the alley in back. The Twenty-third Street end was a clutter of lights and camera equipment with a dais for posing. At the other end of the studio apartment were a kitchen and Hugh's living quarters.

"My kitchen is a set for food- and cookware clients," Hugh explained. "I have Mirro and a couple of others."

"Then I saw your work in *Milady* last month," Ruthana said. "A full-color center spread."

"Did you like it?" Hugh asked.

"It was beautiful."

"Fresh coffee." Hugh poured Ruthana a cup. "Cream and sugar?"

"Please."

They sat across from each other at the kitchen table. Hugh had poured Ruthana's coffee into a mug like his own, lacing it with whipped cream. "I worked at Schraffts on Fifth Avenue when I first came to New York," Hugh said. "They hooked me on whipped cream in my coffee. I understand it's a Viennese habit."

"What did you do?" Ruthana asked.

"I was a busboy," Hugh told her. "Another time I washed dishes, and for a while I was a fry cook."

"When you have a wife, she'll appreciate those talents, Hugh. Where do you come from?"

"Kimball, Nebraska. I thumbed my way here with a Speed Graphic, and not much else. Where is your home?" he asked.

"Philadelphia."

"Mainline I suppose," Hugh said.

"As a matter of fact, yes, but please don't hold it against me."

Hugh laughed. "Prince Rainier certainly didn't hold Mainline Philadelphia against Grace Kelly. I suppose your family knows Grace's?"

"Mother does."

"How did you get into modeling?" Hugh asked.

"I modeled some dresses at a charity fashion show. Shana Deane was there and asked me to join her agency. It was just one of those lucky breaks."

"Shana has a good eye for beauty," Hugh said.

"Thank you." Ruthana wished that she didn't blush so easily. "I worked at Macy's for a while when I started with Shana. It was good experience and helped me get over being too shy."

"The worst job I had was ushering at Radio City Music Hall," Hugh told Ruthana. "I haven't seen a movie since, and the smell of hot-buttered popcorn makes me ill."

Ruthana found Hugh disturbingly attractive, but his easy manner and willingness to share his early job experiences put her at ease. She was here to work in front of his camera. From experience, Ruthana had learned that a graceful body and pretty face were only a part of being a successful model. The rest was hard work and long hours.

"Do you suppose we should start?" Ruthana asked when she'd finished her coffee.

"Yes, we should." Hugh was serious now, and all business. "The suits I want you to wear are laid out in the dressing room. For these test shots I'll use black and white film and a Rollei-flex."

Three walls of the small dressing room, off the studio end of the apartment, were mirrors and gave a model the chance to check her appearance from all angles before going in front of the camera. There was also a lavatory and a dressing table. Hugh was more thoughtful than many photographers Ruthana had posed for. Some dressing rooms were drafty and barely larger than a telephone booth.

In Ruthana's hatbox was a robe to throw on between poses, beach sandals, and a theatrical makeup kit. Ruthana sat at the dressing table to apply just a hint of eye shadow and eyeliner, transparent lipstick, and a hint of rouge.

Hugh had stacked the suits in the order he wanted them worn. On top was Madame Yvonne's briefest bikini. The yellow bottom was handkerchief size, to be kept in place (hopefully) by black tie ribbons, and the skimpy bra was more revealing than concealing. Ruthana had modeled lingerie and swimwear before, but always in a crowded studio or showroom. Today she'd be working alone with Hugh.

Keep your cool, girl, she advised herself.

CHAPTER 2

Once before Ruthana had modeled swimwear for an overweight, bearded satyr who had slyly suggested he would have paid her extra to pose without wearing a suit, a proposition she'd politely turned down. When the yellow bikini was adjusted to her satisfaction, Ruthana wondered if she was getting into a sticky situation. Last night's experience with Alex was still fresh in her mind. Was Hugh as trustworthy as he seemed?

Shana advised her models to always have a

third party present when working lingerie or swimwear. Ruthana found Hugh adjusting lights around the dais.

"Won't you need someone here to help us?" she asked Hugh.

It was the best way she knew to suggest there should be a chaperon. But Hugh gave her a blank look and said, "What did you say?"

"Shana cautions us to have a third party present when we work lingerie or swimwear," Ruthana said with a blush. "It's for your protection, too, in case a girl tries to blackmail you with rape." She hated her prim tone of voice. "Not that I would."

Hugh laughed. "The caretaker's wife, Mrs. Schmidt, can bring her knitting up here," he said, "but I warn you, she talks a mile a minute and gets on my nerves. If you will feel safer with her up here, however, it can be arranged. But I'll take a chance on you not yelling rape, if you'll trust me to keep my hands to myself."

"Mrs. Schmidt would probably drop stitches if she saw what I'm not wearing under this robe," Ruthana said with a smile. "Let's not bother her today."

"Fine." Hugh touched her chin with a finger

to turn Ruthana's face. "Your makeup is just right," he said. "I have to send most girls back to wash their face. You don't slather it on, do you?"

"I try not to."

"Now let me see the suit. Is it warm enough for you? I turned up the thermostat to seventy-five degrees. I'll put it higher if you wish."

"No, this is comfortable." Ruthana took off her robe and laid it on a chair. "Do you like this number? Madame Yvonne didn't waste any material!"

"She certainly didn't," Hugh said. "Yellow is a good color for you. This is what I want you to do, Ruthana." His businesslike manner relaxed Ruthana. "I can't find a body flaw, your legs are great, and there's just enough hip. I want you on the dais, and then to forget I'm here. Yawn, stretch, sit down, stand up, just slip from one pose to the next. Can you work this loosely?"

"I can certainly try," Ruthana said.

"Good. Let's go to work."

On the dais Ruthana patted a genuine yawn, and Hugh snapped the camera for the first time. There were a dozen different styles in Madame

Yvonne's swimwear collection, and Hugh
wanted test black-and-whites of each, so the
morning wore into afternoon without any pause.
Ruthana slipped easily from one pose to another
as Hugh circled the dais, trying various camera
angles. It reminded Ruthana of the ballet train-
ing she'd had as a child.

"Well, I guess that's it," Hugh finally said,
ducking out of the camera strap around his neck.
He stretched and arched his body to ease the
tiredness in the small of his back. "Are you as
tired as I am? We've just put in an eight-hour
day."

"I'm a little tired," Ruthana admitted.

"Hungry, too, I'll bet. We skipped lunch
break. I was going to have the deli over on
Broadway send in some pastrami and corned
beef sandwiches, but we were working together
so well it skipped my mind."

"I'll remember to bring a box lunch next
time," Ruthana said. "I was getting weak."

Hugh laughed. "Since I owe you a meal, I'll
tell you what. There's a casserole in the refrig.
If you'll pop it in the oven and keep an eye on
it, I'll duck into the darkroom and develop a
few rolls."

"Have you salad makings?" Ruthana asked.

"Sure. There are a couple of bottles of champagne in one of those cupboards, and an ice bucket somewhere. Start the champagne chilling. Anything you can't find, sing out. I probably won't know where it is, either."

Ruthana and Hugh had formed an easy relationship as they worked together, and she felt a deep rapport with the man. She was delighted to be working in Hugh's kitchen with all its modern gadgetry.

The casserole was spaghetti and spicy Italian sausage. Ruthana found a cucumber and avocados for her salad, and mixed a thin oil dressing with a touch of garlic. For dessert she found strawberries and whipped cream. Hugh's refrigerator was well stocked with a sprinkling of gourmet foods. It was obvious to Ruthana that here was a bachelor who liked to eat and who spent quite a bit of time in his kitchen.

She found a red-and-white-checked tablecloth and candles on a top cupboard shelf. Hugh kept his apartment and kitchen neat as a pin, but the cupboards were a mess. Spices and canned foods had been stacked in them willynilly. Humming to herself, Ruthana was just finishing with the organization of his cupboards when Hugh emerged from the darkroom.

Hugh whistled softly. "Now I'll never be able to find anything. You're really something else, Ruthana. Those salads look delicious."

The candles were lit, and the champagne cooling.

"Could you find anything in the cupboards before?" Ruthana asked. "You have just about three of every spice and condiment. You could start a grocery store with what's in these cupboards."

"More likely a restaurant," Hugh said. "I took Home Ec in high school, the only boy in the class. I had to make both the football and basketball team to prove I wasn't sissy. I like to cook. Do you know that turns a lot of women off?"

"I don't know why it should," Ruthana told him. "After all, the best chefs are men. I'd want my husband to be at home in my kitchen and, incidentally, you have quite a kitchen here."

"Isn't it? Do you like the eye-level oven? As I told you, I use it in my work and that gives me a tax shelter."

The spaghetti with chopped mushrooms and

anchovies mixed into it was as delicious as it smelled, and Ruthana's salad was a hit, especially the dressing.

Hugh found a dusty bottle of Chianti to drink with their meal, saving the champagne for later.

"Now go smoke your pipe," Ruthana said when they'd finished the strawberries and whipped cream. "I know how to use a dish-washer."

"Can you make espresso?" Hugh asked.

"If you have the right coffee for it."

"Look in one of those bottom cupboards," he said with a grin. "Where you finally found the ice bucket. Don't try to put them in order or you'll be here all night."

When she joined Hugh with the espresso coffee, Ruthana asked, "How did the test shots come out?"

"I'm glad you've finally asked," Hugh said, knocking the ashes out of his pipe. "Another model would have haunted me in the darkroom to see how her pictures came out. Are you really that disinterested? They came out great."

"You would have told me quickly enough if

they hadn't," Ruthana said. "We'd be up at the other end doing retakes right now."

"You have a face, a body, and the poise that makes my work easy," Hugh told Ruthana. "I haven't printed anything yet or I'd show you. You're going to sell Madame Yvonne's swimwear until her factory is swamped with back orders. Ready for some champagne?"

"Yes. That will go very well right now, but then I'll have to go home and finish my packing."

Hugh unwound the wire and popped the cork of one bottle. "Just between us, most models are so taken with themselves they bore me stiff. I think I have two exceptions to the general rule, however, in you and Penny Andrews. Do you know her?"

"No. She works out of another agency. Didn't she do a TV spot for Avondale Cosmetics last fall?" Ruthana asked. "I seem to remember she did."

"That's right," Hugh said. "You and she will be seeing a lot of each other during the next three weeks. I hope the three of us get along. Saba isn't a very large island."

"We'll get along," Ruthana promised.

"As a matter of fact, there were two other girls I could have used for Madame Yvonne's resort wear, but Candy is a pain, and Marsha chases me. I thought you and Penny should hit it off. I've worked with her before. Penny's a bit flaky, but she's a good kid. I'm sure you'll like her."

"I'm flattered, but you didn't have to worry," Ruthana said. "I've worked with Candy and Marsha. They don't bother me."

"You have the patience of a saint if you can get along with Candy," Hugh said.

Hugh was slumped in a leather chair. Ruthana was on a sofa bed, knees drawn up, feet tucked under her. Ruthana sensed that he was seeing her now as a desirable woman and not just another model. He got up to open the second bottle of champagne and filled her glass. Disturbed by his nearness, Ruthana sat up and put her feet on the carpet.

Hugh sat down beside her. His arm rested on the pillows behind Ruthana. Ruthana was aware of him studying her profile while she sipped her champagne. His hand cupped her shoulder. "Finish your champagne," he breathed.

Hugh's touch triggered alarms in Ruthana

because she wanted his kiss and to be held in his arms. When Hugh took her stemmed champagne glass to set it aside, their fingers touched. Ruthana couldn't trust herself.

"I really think I should be going, Hugh," she told him. "I do have a lot of packing, and it's getting late."

When she stood up, Hugh did, too, with a sardonic expression on his face. "I haven't thrown such incomplete a pass since playing grammar school football," he said. "You get your things and I'll call us a cab."

"It was probably my fault you thought it was a passing situation," Ruthana said. "I really do have to go home."

"Not alone," Hugh said in a firm voice. "New York's getting to be a jungle. I've been mugged twice within a few blocks of here."

It was still raining but turning colder. In the cab Hugh said, "While you're packing, remember sweaters. Saba is just a mountaintop sticking up out of the Caribbean. The nights are cold."

"I've never heard of Saba," Ruthana said. "Where is it?"

"It's one of the Leeward Islands of the

Netherlands Antilles. Saba is only about five square miles. It's governed by the Dutch, and I chose it because it's off the beaten track and not cluttered with too many tourists. Little more than a thousand people make their home there, half of them black."

"It sounds as if you've been there before," Ruthana said. "Have you?"

"Yes, a couple of years ago. I took a friend along for what I thought would be a restful week, but she nearly drove me out of my mind. You eat, you sleep, you climb the mountain, and that's about all there is to do on Saba, unless you like people. Have you ever watched a girl polish her nails and pout for a solid week?"

"No." Ruthana laughed. "I don't think I could stand it."

"I did," Hugh told her. "I went up the wall at least once every day. She and I haven't spoken since."

The driver had pulled up in front of Ruthana's building. Hugh came around the car to help her out. "I guess you can make it from here alone," he said.

"It was a good day and a wonderful supper," Ruthana said. "Thank you. I'd ask you up for coffee, but I left my place in a mess getting ready this morning."

"Sure. Another time," Hugh said. "Good night, Ruthana."

Ruthana's phone was ringing when she reached her apartment. It was Roberta Franklin, calling from Philadelphia, and her first question was, "Where in the world have you been all day and half the night, Ruthana? I've been trying to reach you for hours."

The modeling assignment on Saba had come up so recently that Ruthana hadn't yet told her mother not to expect her for the holidays.

"I've been busy on an assignment, Mother."

"Until this hour? I can't believe that. I've called to find out what train you're taking tomorrow, Ruthana. You surely don't intend to fly in the sort of weather we're having. I absolutely forbid it."

"Mother, I won't be coming home this Christmas. I'm flying to the West Indies the day after tomorrow. We'll be shooting the Madame Yvonne collection," Ruthana said. "It's a very important assignment."

"Why that's Christmas Day!" Roberta was scandalized. "You'll just have to cancel your plans because I'm planning a Christmas party and dance for you. The orchestra is already engaged."

"Now, Mother, you had no right to do that. You know I hate parties, and I can't cancel my plans. I'm going to the West Indies."

"Ruthana, you can't do this to me! After all, I am your mother, and what are all my friends going to think? I've been patient with you about this modeling thing, but this is the absolute limit. It's time you began thinking about marriage to an eligible man so you can take your proper place in society."

Ruthana sighed. When her mother got on this subject, she wouldn't be interrupted.

"Alex Farnsworth was going to see you when he went to New York. I hope you weren't too busy to make a good impression on Alex. He's really a sweet boy. I thought you and he would have something to tell me last year, but no. You had to get this modeling thing out of your system. Have you seen Alex?"

"Yes, Mother, the other night, and he's a crashing bore. We had quite a wrestling match, but I got the decision. I don't think he'll bother me again."

"Bother you? I'm shocked, Ruthana. You should be flattered by his attention, you really should. It could be the marriage of the year, and then you can give up this modeling foolishness. Alex will be here in Philadelphia over the holidays. That's another reason you simply must come home."

"Sorry, Mother. I have other plans," Ruthana said. "Maybe I can make it home for Easter."

Since her father died when she was three, Ruthana had been under her mother's thumb, Roberta's only child. The only time Ruthana had gone completely against her mother's wishes was when she came to New York and signed up with the Shana Deane modeling agency. The past year taught Ruthana how she'd been bullied all her life, and she intended to make an end to it.

"Easter!"

"Mother, listen to me carefully. I no longer have to depend on you for money. I make good money as a model, and I like the profession just fine. I'm sorry I didn't tell you sooner I wouldn't be coming home this Christmas, but it couldn't be helped. And I don't want to hear anything more about Alexander Farnsworth, from you or anyone else. I'm twenty-one years old, but not ready yet for marriage. When I am, I'll tell you and introduce you to the man. Good night, Mother."

Ruthana hung up the telephone. It rang almost immediately. She picked it up, expecting an angry diatribe from Roberta Franklin, but it was Alexander Farnsworth's smooth voice.

"I say, I think I should explain the little misunderstanding we had the other evening, Ruthana," he said. "You got a bit emotional, but there's a very simple explanation for my conduct."

"I don't believe I want to hear it, Alex," she said in a cold voice.

"My dear girl! It's all very elemental. A man wants his wife to be a virgin. You've been living alone, and we know about models, don't we? I just wanted to determine whether or not you have round heels before proposing marriage. So you see, there it is, and no reason you should take umbrage."

His effrontery stunned Ruthana. "Let me get this straight, Alex. You tried to rape me just to find out if I'd roll over for any man, is that right?"

"Essentially, yes."

"Having passed that test to your satisfaction, you're now proposing marriage," Ruthana said. "Is this true?"

"Now you have it, Ruthana." He spoke as if he were patronizing a bright child. "We can discuss the wedding plans when you come to Philadelphia tomorrow. Perhaps we'll announce our engagement at the party your mother is giving. I'll speak to her about that. I know she's very much in favor of our match."

"Take your proposal and stuff it, Alex!"

When she'd slammed the telephone back on its cradle, Ruthana sat for a minute, boiling, but then she snickered, only to burst into a wild gale of laughter. Ruthana laughed until tears ran down her cheeks.

CHAPTER 3

The 747 flying from Kennedy Airport to San
Juan, Puerto Rico, on Christmas morning was
only half-filled, because most holiday travelers
had already reached their destinations. Across
the aisle in the first-class section from Penny
Andrews and Ruthana, Hugh Laidman was
studying a book about filters and lenses.

Ruthana had seen Penny on television and
once or twice while making her modeling
rounds. She was a little in awe of Penny's
haughty carriage and classically beautiful face,

and wondered if they could get along for three weeks on a small island as well as she'd indicated to Hugh. But Ruthana discovered she needn't have worried. Penny fairly bubbled with good humor.

"Just think, Ruthana," she said. "Three glorious weeks in the sun to have fun. No rain, no snow, no sleet. In the bargain we get *paid* for it! It sure beats wearing your fingers to the bone on a typewriter, don't you think?"

"I think," Ruthana said. "You're talking to a forty-words-a-minute girl who made straight D in typing. But I suspect we'll earn our keep. Laidman worked me eight straight hours yesterday, making test shots."

"I've heard he's a slave driver," Penny admitted. "But look at that manly profile," she whispered. "Did he make a pass?"

"No. We're quite safe with Laidman."

"What a shame. I was down with some kind of twenty-four-hour bug. But something must have happened between you and Laidman yesterday."

"How did you get that idea?" Ruthana asked.

"The way he kept sneaking looks at you while we had breakfast in the terminal. Come clean,

40

did you turn him on? You can tell me. I only listen to gossip. I don't broadcast any."

"Nothing happened. We just worked and had supper," Ruthana said.

"Look!" Penny leaned across Ruthana to look out the cabin window. "There's a ship down there."

"It looks like a bathtub toy."

"I went on a South American cruise last year with a couple of other girls. Did we have a ball! I think the singles outnumbered the crew. There was this handsome first officer, however, with one of those made-in-England accents." Penny sighed. "Unfortunately, he was happily married."

"Do you have a current boyfriend?" Ruthana asked.

"There's this fellow in Pittsburgh I used to know in high school. He travels for some glass company, and we get together whenever he comes to New York. A nice hometown type. Then there's a pilot on the New York-London run. I met him last summer at a singles bar. I know an artist who thinks he's Michelangelo in his more expansive moments. He's fun when he isn't being paranoid," Penny said. "You might say I play the field these days. What about you?"

"I've been too busy this past year to date very much," Ruthana confessed. "I'm just getting started in modeling."

"I've been at it three years. Pretty soon I'll be doing characters," she laughed. "Miss Snoopy or Mrs. Geriatric."

"I somehow doubt that," Ruthana said. "You say you're from Pittsburgh? We're both Pennsylvanians, because I'm from Philadelphia."

"How about that?" Penny asked. "My father's a steelworker, and proud of it. He and mother raised six of us on wages. What does your father do?"

"He was an investment broker, but he died when I was a small child. I don't remember him very well. My mother, for some reason, never remarried."

"It must have been tough on her bringing you up," Penny said.

"Well, my father left us quite a bit of money, so I guess it wasn't too bad," Ruthana admitted. "She tried pretty hard to spoil me. I was pretty rude to her on the phone the other night, but she keeps trying to marry me off."

Ruthana was surprised to find herself telling Penny Andrews these things. At boarding school it hadn't been easy for her to talk about herself with the other girls.

"Are you into the society thing?" Penny asked. "Mainline and all that?"

"Not really. That's why I got out on my own. It's the best thing I ever did."

"I hand it to you," Penny said. "I'm afraid I'd be inclined to stay in the lap of luxury."

"Not if your mother considered you her prize filly, to be mated with some polo-playing stud," Ruthana told the girl.

Penny's delighted laughter turned the heads of the other passengers and made Hugh look over. Penny flushed and covered her mouth with her hand. "I couldn't help it," she said. "It wasn't what you said so much as it was the way you said it."

Hugh smiled across the aisle at them. It obviously pleased him to see his models getting along so well this early.

The terminal in San Juan was decorated for Christmas but was nearly empty. It would be an hour before their Windward Airlines flight

43

took off for Saba. Hugh invited the girls to have lunch in the airport restaurant.

"Windward only serves chewing gum," he explained.

Waiting for their orders, Ruthana asked Hugh, "How did Saba get its name?"

The only other customer in the restaurant was at the counter, with his back toward them.

"It's supposed to be named after the Queen of Sheba," Hugh said. "I don't know if there's any truth in that or not."

The man at the counter swung around on his stool, and his eyes met Ruthana's. The surprise on his dark face was unmistakable.

He acts as if I'm a ghost, Ruthana thought.

The man shook his head slightly, as if to clear it, then palmed a tip on the counter for his waitress, and came to their table.

A powder-blue shirt was open to the waist, the V exposing a hairless chest, with a gold medallion in the hollow of his throat. He was extremely handsome, looking like the head on an ancient Roman coin, but there was stubbornness in his face and the hint of sardonic impudence in his almost black eyes.

He spoke to all of them, but stared at Ruthana. "I could not help myself from overhearing mention of my island," he said. "Saba was as remote as her land in early days, so it is named for Sheba. May I sit?"

Hugh questioned the girls with a glance. When they nodded, Hugh said, "Please do. Will you have some coffee?"

"No, thank you. I am Philipe Simon."

Hugh introduced himself and the girls.

"We Sabans are a curious mixture, even for the Caribbean," Philipe said. "Whites descend from shipwrecked sailors and buccaneers, with a few colonists from Holland, England, Scotland, France, and Sweden. You see, Saba has changed hands thirteen or fourteen times since Columbus first saw it. But I think you'll find us very friendly people, the blacks and whites alike. We don't get many tourists."

"We're not exactly tourists," Hugh said and explained their purpose in coming to Saba.

"Excellent!" Philipe smiled at Ruthana. "You must visit my sister, Celeste, and me. You'll be staying at Sam Lord's Castle?"

Hugh admitted they would be. He was becoming resentful of Philipe's overwhelming interest in Ruthana. "We're going to be quite busy," he said. "There won't be much time for socializing."

"There is always time on Saba," Philipe told them. He got up. "I won't disturb you further."

He left the restaurant.

"Wow!" was Penny's comment. "I wonder if there are any other Sabans like him. I thought he was going to use that Haven't-we-met-before? line on you, Ruthana. How do you do it?"

"I don't remember Simon or his sister from my last visit," Hugh said, "and he's a guy you'd remember. Philipe Simon sounds French."

"So does Celeste," Penny said. "I wonder what she's like. I can hardly wait to find out."

"I'm sure we'll see more of Philipe and meet his sister," Hugh said. "You say good morning to a Saban, and the first thing you know you're in his house meeting the family."

Their flight to Saba was called over the public-address system.

The twin-engine aircraft was propeller driven and seated only ten passengers. The whole airplane could have been fitted inside the 747, with space left over for a hundred passengers.

"That contraption is a museum piece!" Penny

exclaimed. "Do you suppose they rent parachutes?"

"We could have gone down on the mailboat," Hugh said. "The trouble there is that Saba doesn't have a harbor. Natives wade out and carry you in through the surf. Besides, the boat only runs once a week."

"We're really going back yonder, aren't we?" Ruthana said. "This is fun."

Seated in the airplane, they discovered they were the only passengers. There was no air conditioning. The cabin quickly became an oven.

"What's holding us on the ground?" Hugh asked when the Dutch pilot came back through the cabin.

The pilot was an older man, with a brushy gray crewcut, a ruddy face, and a genial grin. "We're flying down Saba's new administrator today," he said. "He's on the phone with Her Royal Majesty." He tipped back his cap to mop his forehead. "Hot for Christmas, isn't it? KLM reports it's snowing in Holland."

"It had begun to snow in New York before we left," Ruthana said.

The pilot nodded. "We picked up Pan Am asking about conditions there. Well, here comes our new administrator. I guess we'd better get this bird ready to fly."

Philipe Simon entered the cabin, ducking his dark head to get through the door. "Take her up, Hans," he said to the pilot and slipped into an empty seat beside Ruthana. "I suppose he told you I was talking to the queen."

"He did drop her name," Ruthana acknowledged.

Philipe chuckled. "It was no one in Holland as important as that. I just had a few last-minute questions to ask De Graaf, our last Dutch administrator."

The airplane had rushed down the runway and now was sliding up through the sky over the blue Caribbean. "Would it very much surprise you if I were to tell you that Celeste has painted your portrait?" Philipe asked Ruthana.

"Very much, since I've never visited your island, nor have I met your sister," Ruthana said. This man disturbed her. But she couldn't yet say why.

Hugh and Penny were in the seats behind them, and Ruthana was sure they'd tuned their ears to this conversation she was having with

Philipe. To change the subject, she asked, "Are you elected or appointed?"

"Appointed by Her Royal Majesty. She granted me an audience while I was in Holland. I speak French better than I do Dutch, so she was gracious enough to converse with me in that language. Before my appointment we've had a new Dutchman every two years. Saba was sort of a Dutch Siberia. They couldn't wait to go home from our little island."

"Were you born on Saba?" Ruthana asked.

"Yes. Both my sister and I. We're twins. Our father was Dutch, our mother French. You'll hear that she is a *bruja*."

"I don't understand," Ruthana said.

Hugh spoke up from behind them. "A *bruja* is a Voodoo witch."

"Wow!" Penny said.

"You'll learn that Celeste has some kind of Power," Philipe said.

"I'm not a superstitious person," Ruthana said in a prim voice.

Philipe laughed. "You will be."

"Tell us about Saba," Penny prompted from behind them.

Philipe hung his arm over the back of the

seat. "We have just six miles of roads on Saba, every inch carved out of the side of the mountain. Most of our men go to sea, because there's little else they can do, and Sabans are excellent sailors. We have goats, and a nightclub, The Lido. Every Saturday night there's a jukebox dance at The Lido. We have a few rocky beaches."

"That's why I selected Saba," Hugh said. "I want to catch the flavor of the island. It's a backdrop you wouldn't believe."

The airplane was making its final approach to Saba. Literally, it was a mountaintop poking up out of the Caribbean, an extinct volcano. Ruthana gasped when she saw the landing field. From the air it looked the size of a tablecloth, with a sheer cliff on one side, a straight drop to the pounding surf on the other. As small as the airplane had seemed at first, now it looked to be too large to land there.

Ruthana stiffened.

"Wow!" Penny breathed. "We try to land *there*?"

"Close your eyes," Hugh said.

Philipe's hand grasped Ruthana's. "Hans could

land this thing on a handkerchief," he told her in a low voice.

"And he's just about to do it!" she groaned.

The landing gear swung down, wheels skipped across grass, and then they were rolling out.

Hugh, Penny, and Ruthana heaved a sigh of relief. She slipped her hand out of Philipe's. "I think I just swallowed my heart," she said.

Ruthana, in the panic of landing, had jerked her seat belt too tight. Now she couldn't unbuckle it.

"Let me," Philipe said.

Philipe pressed the buckle, and Ruthana was free. Returning blood circulation put pins and needles in her thighs and calves.

Her face was inches from his. It was utterly outrageous, but his hands cupped her face, and his lips met Ruthana's. It was a lingering kiss. "Welcome back to Saba, Katerina," Philipe whispered. Then he was gone.

Ruthana brushed the salty taste of his kiss from her lips with the back of her hand.

"It would seem you've made a conquest, Franklin," Hugh said with heavy sarcasm, and his smile was tight. "We're down here to work. You're not being paid to romance the locals."

"Stop being so darned gross, Laidman!" It was Penny coming to her rescue. "Franklin didn't encourage the guy, although I wouldn't blame her if she had."

Hugh apologized. "I just don't like Simon," he said. "Sorry if I jumped on you."

"I don't like him, either," Ruthana told Hugh.

Up to a point this was true. But Ruthana didn't add that Philipe Simon frightened her.

Sam Lord watched the plane come in and land. Hugh had mailed their reservations a month ago. Sam remembered Hugh Laidman faintly, but the spoiled girl with green eyes and pouting lips Hugh had brought with him, vividly. She'd called him Sammie, a name he hated, but she was a bored female guest of Sam Lord's Castle.

Sam Lord hoped Hugh had chosen better partners this time. "My God, at least they're younger," Sam said to himself. "Where does this guy find them?"

It was five years ago that Sam bought his castle. He was tired after fighting a dozen small wars and two big ones. "It's time I put my feet up and watched a few sunsets," he'd told Lydia.

Where was she now? Sam didn't wonder, and he didn't much care. It was worth the money she'd stolen to be rid of her.

Sam Lord was fifty his last birthday. He wore an Australian bush hat, with a pinned-up brim, and a bush jacket that covered the .45 he always wore on his right hip. The hard feel of that heavy weapon gave him confidence. And who knew? Saba was off the beaten track far enough to be safe, but who really knew? A man with mortal enemies from Singapore to Timbuktu couldn't be too careful.

Standing beside his Jeep, Sam squinted into the sun as Hugh, Penny, and Ruthana came toward him. "Where *does* this guy find them?" he asked himself a second time.

Sam shaded his gray eyes with a hand to see the honey-blonde better. "Just a girl baby!" he muttered.

The other girl walked with self-assurance. No problem there. She was pretty enough, too, but hands off.

"This is Penny Andrews and Ruthana Franklin," Hugh Laidman was saying. "You got my letter?"

So Ruthana was the girl baby.

"You're my only guests this week, Mr. Laidman," Sam Lord said, with a grin. "Business is slow this time of year. I not only got your letter, reserving rooms, but I framed it."

Sam told the girls, "Welcome to Saba and Sam Lord's Castle." He took off his hat to make a sweeping bow. "Seldom am I honored with such beautiful guests."

White hair contrasted with Sam's deeply tanned face. Ruthana sensed Sam was taking more than a passing interest in her and thought, *My father would have been his age.*

CHAPTER 4

The road down to Windwardside and Sam Lord's Castle had been carved out of bedrock and was one switchback after another. Sam drove the Jeep with Ruthana in the front seat beside him.

"Did you have a comfortable flight?" he asked her.

Ruthana nodded. "Very nice. It's a pleasure to get away from New York at this time of year. We heard it's snowing up there now."

Sam admired the way she carried her head.

"I haven't seen a flake of snow for ten years," he said. This girl really was a princess! "It gets cold here some nights but it never snows."

Sam slowed the Jeep because a billy goat was nibbling grass in the middle of the road. "Gangway, Clarence," he called instead of honking the horn.

The goat looked up with a baleful stare.

"Come on, Clarence, move," Sam coaxed.

The goat took a last bite of grass before he minced off the road. Stolidly chewing, he watched them pass.

"Somebody's pet?" Hugh asked.

"Everybody's pet in Windwardside," Sam told him. "Last week he ambled into our kitchen and ate the curtains before Sable could run him off. Sable is our cook. She makes a mean goat stew, and Clarence knows it."

"He looks like king of the mountain," Penny said, looking back over her shoulder. "I think he's cute."

"He's been known to butt, so watch out if Clarence comes around," Sam told her. "Whatever you do, don't turn your back and lean over. My last lady guest who did that couldn't sit down for a week."

* * *

When they entered the small village of Windwardside, Ruthana was entranced. Small houses with narrow windows lined each side of the road, and every house was protected by a stone wall.

"This is like something out of the Brothers Grimm!" she exclaimed. "Look there, Penny. Each home has graves in front of it."

"There isn't enough level ground on Saba to have a cemetery," Sam explained. Stopping, he backed the Jeep to let a Volkswagen pass. "We run to bugs and Jeeps because cars have to be rafted ashore. A few are still out there on the bottom."

"What about building materials?" Hugh asked.

"Same thing. We don't have anything that even looks like a harbor. I lost half a ton of cement in the surf last week."

Sam Lord's Castle, dating from the 1700s and once a Dutch governor's mansion, was built in the shape of a U, with a restaurant and bar in the shaded patio between the two wings. It stood on a cliff overlooking the sea.

The room reserved for Ruthana and Penny

was a large one, with four-poster beds and a lazy, wide-bladed ceiling fan to stir the air.

"Wow!" Penny bounced on her bed. "Three weeks of this is going to spoil me rotten."

Supper that evening was broiled lobster, drawn in butter and served on a bed of seaweed.

The only other guest currently staying at The Castle was Arthur Teach, a retired English headmaster. "Arthur has been with me the past five years, ever since I bought this place," Sam told them at the supper table. "He helped me lay down my wines."

Arthur inclined his head. "Quite so. I'm afraid my American host didn't know the difference between a dry Spanish sherry and Château Lafite."

"Hey, I though Lafite was a pirate," Penny said. "I never knew he was a wine."

"Jean Laffite was the pirate," Arthur pointed out. "The Lafite winemakers may be distantly related. I find that an interesting point. I'll have to look it up." He polished his monocle. "Did you know there are two ways to spell that name?" Arthur asked Penny.

"No, sir, I didn't know that," Penny said, and her chagrin about the joke that had misfired amused Ruthana.

"There are, you know. With two *f*'s or with only one. I believe the pirate preferred his name spelled with a single *f*, as witnessed in his personal journal, which a relative recently published. Historians, however, use the double *f*."

"Anything you want to know about Saba or any West Indies island," Sam said, "ask Arthur. He's a walking history book."

"My American host flatters me," Arthur said, but he was pleased. With a twinkle in his eye, he told Penny, "I did find your little joke amusing."

"Thank you, I think," she said.

Sable was a ponderous woman with skin like black satin and a smile that revealed spaced, very white teeth. She wore a towering white chef's cap, a gift from Arthur. The maid who served them, Katche, was slender and brown-skinned. A red chignon was knotted on her head, and long gold loops swung from her ears.

"Katche's husband is a sailor," Sam told them. "Sabans are the best sailors in the world. There's no other way to make a living here. Saba's is a postal money-order economy."

It was chilly in the patio, with the sun down, and Ruthana was grateful that Hugh had suggested she pack sweaters. Penny hadn't been that fortunate, so she wore a sweater borrowed from Ruthana.

As they sat around the table, sipping dark rum punches, Sam got up and lit a hurricane lantern. "One minute until lights out," he said.

Arthur explained that the island's generator was always shut down at eleven o'clock.

When he excused himself, so did Hugh. "Sam and I go looking for locations at daybreak," Hugh told the girls. "We'll be gone most of the day, so you girls are on your own tomorrow. Don't fall off the mountain."

Sam went to the bar to make fresh drinks. "I see Philipe Simon flew down with you today," he said when he'd returned to the table. "What do you think of our new administrator?"

"Very nice looking," Penny said.

Ruthana had waited all evening for the subject of Philipe Simon to come up. "Where does he live on Saba?" she asked.

"Over at Bottom. Which really isn't the bottom, because it's on a cliff, like Windwardside, but it's almost flat. Philipe and his twin sister, Celeste, live together in an old house built by a pirate."

"Do you think he'll be a good administrator?" Ruthana asked Sam.

"I don't know." Sam's was a guarded answer. "Philipe's the first native-born Saban the Dutch trust with their island. De Graaf was a good man until he was hexed off Saba."

"Hexed?" Ruthana said. "That sounds medieval!"

Sam's eyes met Ruthana's, and he was serious. "Black or white, Sabans are superstitious, and I've learned the hard way not to take some of their superstitions lightly. Let me tell you about De Graaf. When he came out from Holland a year ago, he was a genial Dutchman, but he had some ideas for Saba and the Sabans. One idea was to kill off some of these local superstitions, like the fear of *jumbies*."

"Just what is a *jumbie*?" Ruthana asked.

"It's a spirit of the dead."

"A zombie, like they have on Haiti?" Penny asked.

Sam shook his head. "No. Zombies are the

living dead. Arthur has an interesting theory about them, by the way. Ask him for it sometime. *Jumbies* are dead spirits trying to come back among the living. At night they try to move in where they used to live. Just about every house on Saba is closed up at night to keep out the *jumbies*. De Graaf was going to change all that. He considered the lack of night air a health hazard."

"I should think it would be," Penny said.

Sam nodded. "I guess it is. We have quite a few tubercular cases among the poor. Anyway, De Graaf crossed Celeste Simon when he got on her about selling charms. The next thing we knew his health began to fail. He began tossing down too much Dutch gin, and having hallucinations. De Graaf used to come here often, and I knew him well. Doctors over on Saint Martin couldn't find a thing wrong with him."

"What kind of hallucinations?" Ruthana asked. "The man sounds mentally ill."

"Maybe pink elephants from the gin," Penny suggested. "I had an uncle that used to get D.T.'s."

"Here on Saba, De Graaf claimed *jumbies* followed him wherever he went." Sam pointed to a chair across the patio. "One used to sit right over there when De Graaf sat where I am now."

Penny stole a glance at the empty chair. "Did you see him?" she asked Sam.

"No. He was De Graaf's *jumbie*, so I couldn't see him, but De Graaf would convince you he was there. Finally he gave up his post, recommended that Philipe be appointed, and fled back to Holland. Every Saban believes Celeste Simon is a *bruja* and bewitched De Graaf. I'll tell you something else. He believes she did, too, and that's going pretty far for a hardheaded Dutchman. I got a letter just the other day from De Graaf. He's in excellent health now and rid of *jumbies*."

"What do you believe?" Ruthana asked.

"That Celeste Simon is a witch."

Ruthana laughed. "You're sending us up now."

"No, I'm not. I fought in the Congo and saw some things there I can't explain. Before De Graaf came, I tangled with Celeste Simon. I thought she'd overcharged one of my guests for a painting and called her on it. Within a month the kitchen caught fire twice; a guest fell out of a second-floor window and broke his leg, claiming someone he didn't see pushed him; and a bottle of whiskey exploded, darned near blinding my barkeeper. Whiskey! Not a carbonated drink."

"What did you do?" Penny asked.

"Sneaked over to Saint Martin and bought this." Sam showed the girls a small leather sack, tied around his neck with a thong. "I was afraid to ask what's in it, but I haven't had an accident since."

"Wow!" Penny said. "I believe."

"It was Philipe Simon who advised me to get the *gris-gris*," Sam confessed.

"That sounds like a put-up job," Ruthana said.

Sam grinned. "You're a little Miss Doubting Thomas, aren't you?"

Ruthana blushed. "I'm not superstitious, if that's what you mean."

"Just be sure you don't cross Celeste Simon while you're here with us on Saba," Sam counseled. "I'm perfectly serious, Ruthana."

"I doubt that I will even meet the woman," Ruthana said, but she shivered.

It was raining when Ruthana woke up the next morning. December and July, she would learn, are the only two months during the year when it rains on Saba. Penny was still asleep. Ruthana dressed in slacks and a sweater to go down to breakfast alone.

"Good morning," Arthur Teach greeted her. "You, too, rise quite early, I see."

"It's a working-girl habit, Mr. Teach. That melon looks delicious."

"With lime juice it is." He clapped his hands for Katche. "A melon for Miss Franklin, please."

"Coffee, too," Ruthana called after the girl.

"Yes, sir. Yes, miss."

"Sleep well?" Arthur asked.

"Very. Sam's rum punches are potent."

"Saba is famous for its dark rum," Arthur told her. "Dark rum and wide-brim straw hats that the women weave. It is a curious little island. Doctor Crossley who worked with Sir Fleming to describe and name penicillin was a Saban. Doctor Howard Hassell, who helped J. R. Oppenheimer perfect your atom bomb, was a Saban. Back in 1920 a Captain Johnson from Saba saved an American submarine and all her crew, under impossible conditions. Saban captains are recognized as the best all over the world, as are Saba's sailors."

"We were talking about Saba's superstitions last night," Ruthana said.

"Ah." Arthur smiled.

Katche brought Ruthana's coffee and melon. "The man, Philipe Simon, has come asking for you, Miss Franklin," she said. "He is waiting outside. Shall I ask him to come here?"

Ruthana's heart jumped. Arthur Teach was watching her with narrowed eyes. "Speak of the devil," he said. "You did mention Saba's superstitions," he reminded the girl. "Philipe and Celeste are believed to have the Power."

"Ask him if he'll join me for coffee," Ruthana told Katche.

"Yes, miss." Katche was nervous and excited.

Philipe wore dark blue trousers, tucked into hiking boots, and a dark blue pullover sweater this morning. His only concession to the rain was a Saban straw hat. A white silk scarf was knotted around his throat.

"My coffee with rum," he instructed Katche.

Avoiding his glance and without answering, Katche scurried into the kitchen. Sable was peering out the kitchen door.

"You two will excuse me?" Arthur said.

Philipe nodded. "Good morning, sir." When

he was gone, Philipe told Ruthana, "Since you won't be working today, perhaps you'll join my sister and me for a lunch."

Penny picked that moment to enter the patio. She pointed to the canvas drawn over it. "I wondered what we do when it rains. Hello, Philipe." She sat at the table with him and Ruthana. "I'm starved!"

Katche had brought his coffee. Penny ordered bacon, eggs, toast, and a melon.

"My sister would like both of you girls for a lunch," Philipe said. Ruthana wondered if Penny would have been included if she hadn't come down to breakfast. "We live over in Bottom. You will see something of our small island on the way."

"Sounds fine to me," Penny said. "What about you, Ruthana?"

"I'd like very much to meet your sister," Ruthana said.

"Good." Philipe smiled and finished his coffee. "I'll wait outside in my car."

"Well, Philipe didn't kiss and run," Penny said in a cheerful voice. "Now we get to meet his sister, the witch. Do you want to bet their ancestors weren't pirates?"

"I'm afraid I'd lose," Ruthana said. She was remembering yesterday's kiss, his mention that Celeste had painted her portrait (impossible!), and that he'd called Ruthana Katerina. "The man does manage to leave an impression," she told Penny. "If it's a line he hands out, it's a new one."

"If he wasn't so attracted to you, I'd make a play for Philipe," Penny said.

"Don't let me be the one to stop you," Ruthana told Penny. "Something about that man scares me."

Philipe's car was an old-model Volkswagen with a canvas top. Ruthana managed to get into the back seat so Penny would ride beside Philipe. They drove around the mountain, through a settlement called Hell's Gate.

"Mount Scenery over there is an extinct volcano," Philipe pointed out. "At least we all hope it is. The mountain does give us hot springs."

Ruthana noticed the lack of young men in both Windwardside and Hell's Gate. "Where are they?" she asked Philipe. "The young men I mean."

"Out at sea or working in the oil refineries on

Aruba or Curaçao. It's always been that way with Sabans. We like to roam."

"Sort of hard on their womenfolk, isn't it?" Penny said. "I'd prefer a live-in husband."

"Don't marry down here, then," Philipe cautioned. "Only the cripples and aged stay home the year round."

The house Philipe shared with his sister was smaller than Ruthana had thought it would be, perched on a cliff jutting out into the sea. Made from yellow brick, it had slit-like windows that could be shuttered during a hurricane.

"A pirate built this place, but a later Dutch governor took it away from him," Philipe said. "The pirate came back here and, for revenge, kidnapped the governor's daughter, Katerina. Our house is haunted, of course." Philipe said it in a matter-of-fact voice. "The Dutchman died in it after his daughter was stolen. When she finally got back to Saba, it was to find that her father and the man she loved were both dead. She killed herself in this house."

Celeste Simon greeted them in the gloomy living room of the old house.

Celeste Simon shocked Ruthana, because

she'd assumed that Philipe and his sister were identical twins, but the woman was much darker than her brother. She was as beautiful as he was handsome, but her features were Negroid. Celeste's eyes were dark pools of uncertain depth.

Ruthana had to drop her eyes when Celeste stared, unblinking, into her face, searching it.

"I've told you about her," Philipe said to his sister.

Celeste nodded. "Katerina."

CHAPTER 5

Philipe said, "Your portrait is in the next room, Ruthana. Would you like to see it before or after we've had our lunch?"

"Let's see it now," Penny urged. "Curiosity is eating me up."

"I feel you two are playing some sort of cat-and-mouse game with me," Ruthana told Philipe and Celeste. "Haven't you forgotten to tell me the rules?"

"I assure you this is no game," Celeste said. "If you knew us better you would realize that."

"It's a very real and puzzling thing that has happened," Philipe added. "We count on you to help us solve the mystery."

"If there's a mystery, let's see this portrait of me now," Ruthana said. "Too much curiosity always spoils my appetite."

The next room to the living room had been made into a studio for Celeste as well as a gallery in which to hang her paintings. Framed Saba scenes and seascapes lined the walls; there wasn't a portrait among them. But there was a large unframed painting on an easel, covered with a white cloth. It was Celeste who removed the cloth. "This was Katerina."

Ruthana heard Penny gasp and drew in her own breath. She was staring at a full-length portrait of the governor's daughter, robed in funeral black with a white flower clasped to her breast. The girl's eyes were downcast, and her face unutterably sad, with blonde hair falling about her shoulders.

What astounded Ruthana was that she felt as if she were looking into a mirror. Celeste, somehow, *had* painted her portrait! The likeness sent her heart racing.

Philipe and Celeste waited for her to comment.

"It's just incredible," was all Ruthana managed to say.

"It's really spooky!" Penny said. "How did you do it?" she asked Celeste.

"Ruthana lived in this house once as Katerina," Celeste said. "We found a cameo brooch with her profile under mysterious circumstances."

"Celeste had urged me to give away an old coat I hadn't worn for years," Philipe told them. "We found the cameo in one of the pockets."

"Katerina came to me in a dream that night," Celeste went on. "In the morning I was compelled to start painting her portrait, and here she is. I don't know what it means."

"It's the only portrait Celeste has ever done," Philipe told Ruthana and Penny. "She was a madwoman until it was finished."

Celeste nodded agreement. "I've never been so driven by some force I couldn't understand, but it is very simple to me now."

In a minute I'll start to believe her! This thought was followed by another. *Witches cast*

spells, and that's what she's doing to me now,
Ruthana told herself.

"Ruthana is Katerina reincarnated," Celeste
said. "You do believe in reincarnation, don't
you?" she asked the girls.

"Yes, I do now," Penny said.

"No," Ruthana told Celeste. "All of us have a
double somewhere."

"And your double just happened to come to
me in a dream?" Celeste's was a superior smile.
"If you believe that, you'll believe anything."

"Do you get any of the fashion magazines?"
Ruthana asked. "I've posed for quite a few ads
in those."

"I don't get them, nor do I read them,"
Celeste said. "Isn't this true, Philipe?"

"That's quite true." The dialogue between
Ruthana and Celeste amused him. "We only
subscribe to Sunday's *The New York Times*."

"As you see, my taste in clothes is simple,"
Celeste said.

Ruthana admired the hand-printed silk shift,
with its classic lines, and thought: Simple, yes,
but very expensive.

"Do you have any Dutch ancestors?" Philipe
asked her.

Her father had been of English descent, but Ruthana knew there were Pennsylvania Dutch on her mother's side of the family, thrifty but poor farming people whose existence Roberta chose to ignore. Faced with Philipe's question, she wanted to lie.

Ruthana found she couldn't. "Yes," she said.

He smiled and spread his hands, as if what she'd just said explained everything.

"But I still don't believe in reincarnation," Ruthana said stubbornly.

"We don't argue with our guests, Philipe." There was that superior smile again. "Our lunch is ready."

Lunch was served by a slight Chinese houseboy Philipe addressed as Chang. Celeste had prepared the dishes herself.

"I have too many enemies on Saba to employ a cook," she told Ruthana and Penny. "*Obeah* is a very real thing in these islands."

"*Obeah*?" Penny asked in a puzzled voice.

"Another name for Voodoo," Philipe explained. "But there's nothing supernatural about poison."

The light green chilled soup was like nothing

Ruthana had ever tasted. "What in the world do you put into this?" she asked Celeste. "I've never tasted anything so delicious!"

"With your career, you find time to cook?" Celeste asked.

"I find the time," Ruthana said. "I'd really like your recipe."

"It's quite simple. You need avocados, milk, ground white-bread crumbs, and champagne. The rest of the ingredients are lemon juice, white sugar, mace, and whipped cream. I'll have Philipe bring you my recipe, if you wish."

"I'd like that very much," Ruthana said.

After the soup the houseboy served shrimp that had been dipped in a sauce made from eggs, flour, baking powder, salt, and a cup and a half of beer before they were fried in shortening. Celeste promised Ruthana a copy of this recipe also.

After lunch Philipe drove Ruthana and Penny from Bottom to Fort Bay, to watch Sabans in their boats bringing in cargo from an anchored freighter. Ruthana found it a suspenseful, thrilling sight. The boats, similar to those she'd seen used by lifeguards at Jones Beach, were rowed by husky boys, and steered by a man with a long sweep oar. The boys would pull with all their might to get the boat into the surf, then ship their oars and take a wet roller-coaster ride to the beach. The man handling the sweep oar, standing in the stern, was entirely responsible for the last rush to the shore.

Doubling back to Bottom, they met Sam and Hugh standing beside Sam's Jeep. It was Sam who flagged them down.

"I guess my fuel pump is shot," he told Philipe. "I've got a spare back at The Castle. Do you suppose you could run it out for me?"

"No trouble," Philipe said.

Sam thanked him. "Ask Arthur Teach, if he's there. He knows where I keep spare parts."

The morning rain had stopped, but heavy clouds still rolled across Saba, burying the mountain tops in their dense mist. "Will you be able to work tomorrow?" Philipe asked Hugh.

"I think so, but we're going to need horses to get us and my equipment to some of these locations I've found today."

"You can rent them in Windwardside," Philipe said.

Hugh nodded. "So Sam Lord tells me."

Penny decided to stay with Sam and Hugh

while they waited for Philipe to bring the fuel pump. "I'm just a third wheel with you and Philipe," she confided to Ruthana. "The man's been devouring you with his eyes all day. I'm afraid inviting me to lunch was an afterthought. He would have preferred showing you off to his sister without me as a chaperon."

"So you throw me to the wolf in Philipe!" Ruthana said. "Some kind of friend you are."

Penny grinned. "For this unselfish gesture on my part, I demand a blow-by-blow account tonight. I don't play Cupid often."

Ruthana wouldn't admit it to Penny, but she welcomed the ride back to Windwardside alone with Philipe, if only to sort out her feelings about the man. It had been a strange day. She was deeply disturbed by Celeste's painting of Katerina and sought an ulterior motive, but could find none. She herself hadn't known she was coming to Saba until only a few days before they departed New York.

The Franklin fortune was considerable, and she was her mother's only heir, so Roberta had coached her well on the subject of fortune hunters. But she was a total stranger to Philipe and his sister! Her chance encounter with him in San Juan was certainly a random thing.

Ruthana made a mental note to ask Sam Lord about Philipe's financial status, if she could do it with discretion.

Their drive on the narrow road back to Bottom was a silent one. Philipe seemed lost in his thoughts as much as she was in her own. Yet there was nothing strained about their silence.

"We'll stop for a minute at home," Philipe said, when they'd entered Bottom. "Celeste will have those recipes you wanted."

"Good. I somehow forgot to thank her for such a lovely lunch."

In a cramped, back-slanted hand, Celeste had written out both recipes and wasn't surprised that Ruthana had returned alone with Philipe. As an excuse to see Katerina's portrait again, Ruthana expressed interest in some of Celeste's other paintings. It wasn't entirely a feigned interest, either. Ruthana had glimpsed a seascape painted at Fort Bay that she wanted for her apartment, and a Hell's Gate street scene with an appealing black urchin she thought would be a good make-up present with Roberta.

She'd noticed the prices on Celeste's paintings for sale were $35 and $40.

Katerina's painting was covered again with the white cloth. When she'd selected the two paintings she wanted and dug in her handbag for money, Philipe held her wrist.

"Your money isn't good today," he said and reached for his own billfold.

"Oh, come on, now!" Ruthana protested. "I can't accept such an expensive present, Philipe."

"I'm no longer a stranger, I hope," he said. "As the new administrator of Saba, I order you to accept these paintings."

"He leaves you no choice," Celeste said.

Philipe paid his sister in guilders.

Ruthana hesitated to ask, but Celeste, when she'd wrapped the paintings, lifted the cloth that covered Katerina. The likeness was even more startling than the first time Ruthana saw the portrait. Looking at it again, she gave her head a puzzled shake.

"Nothing like this has ever happened to me before," she said. "I don't pretend to understand it. You must be psychic," she told Celeste. "What do you intend to do with this portrait?"

"That is up to Philipe." Celeste regarded Ruthana steadily, and there was a glint of hostility in the depth of her eyes. "I would destroy it, but the matter is out of my hands."

"We'd better go get that fuel pump," Philipe said. "I don't want to be on the road after dark."

When they'd left Bottom for Windwardside, Philipe said, "My sister has always been a jealous person. I am, too," he admitted to Ruthana. "This Laidman, what is he to you, Ruthana?"

"Hugh is a photographer. I am a model."

Philipe was watching the road. He slowed as it rose into a cloud, then dipped again. "How long have you known him?" Philipe asked.

"Only for a few days." Philipe was assuming she'd readily answer these personal questions, Ruthana knew, and there was an intensity in the man that frightened Ruthana, even as it attracted her to him. "How well I know Hugh isn't really your concern, is it?" She kept her voice light. "We hardly know each other."

"About that, you're very wrong," Philipe said.

"Do you believe in the Muslim concept of fate, or kismet?"

"I can't say I really do," Ruthana answered. "I like to think that I, alone, control my future and rule my emotions."

Philipe drove the Volkswagen at a snail's pace. They passed through Saint Johns. Above the village a Saban woman waited beside the road and raised her hand to stop the car. Philipe groaned as he put on the brakes.

"I'm about to be reminded that I'm the new administrator on Saba," he told Ruthana.

When he'd stopped the car, Philipe got out to face the stocky woman in a wide-brimmed Saban straw hat. "Mrs. Guder, my companion is a Miss Franklin, one of our guests from New York," he said.

Mrs. Guder gave Ruthana the briefest nod.

"It is my husband again," Mrs. Guder said, without any preamble. "He went to work in the oil refinery on Aruba a month ago, but there hasn't been a florin or guilder on the mailboat for me."

"What do you want me to do, Mrs. Guder?" Philipe asked in a pleasant voice.

"Put him in jail." The woman's mouth was a

hard line, and her eyes were venomous. "He's probably found another black girl over there. Hasn't his wife the right to see him in jail?"

"I'm not sure that she has," Philipe temporized. "I will send a message to Aruba, however. I'm sure there will be money when the mailboat comes next week. In the meantime. . . ." Philipe reached for his billfold, but Mrs. Guder raised her hand to stop him.

"I want *his* money, not charity from you and your sister. Thank you very much."

Turning her back, she marched through the gateway in the stone fence, slamming the wrought-iron gate behind her, and into the small house without so much as a backward glance.

Back in the car Philipe said, "She never would have approached De Graaf this way." He sighed. "The stiff-necked Dutch had their place on Saba."

Ruthana laughed. "How did you come to take the job, Philipe?"

"Celeste insisted."

There was a sharp left turn in the road ahead where it crossed a ridge, with a sheer drop from either side. When they had reached this part of the road that morning, Penny had remarked, "Wow! Somebody could get killed here."

"People have been," Philipe had told her.

A drifting cloud kissed the ridge and passed, but the concrete was wet and puddled. Making the blind short left turn, Philipe turned his head to say something to Ruthana.

"Look out!"

Ahead of them Clarence was nibbling at the grass poking up through a crack in the road.

Philipe stood on the brakes.

The Volkswagen slued on the wet pavement, as Clarence, with a nimble jump, got out of the way. The rear wheels grazed the right-hand shoulder, lost traction. Philipe sawed the steering wheel.

Rear tires kicked a shower of gravel over the cliff on that side of the road. That night Ruthana would tell Penny, "I wondered how many days it would be before someone found our bodies in the smashed Volks at the bottom of that cliff!"

Tires grabbed.

They were safe, and Clarence ambled out into the road behind them to taste the grass again. Across the ridge Philipe pulled off the road.

Ruthana was slumped forward, trembling hands covering her face. She felt his fingers close on her wrists, to draw her hands apart, then straightened, but only to be folded in his arms and pressed to his chest.

"I'm so sorry!" he crooned to her.

Then her face was in his hands, and Philipe's lips crushed her mouth. Ruthana responded immediately to the urgency of his kiss, and the hard warmth of his body. For a moment there was nothing Ruthana could deny Philipe. She was safe from death, and in his strong arms.

Ruthana broke away from Philipe and turned her face to rest her hot forehead against the cool glass of the car window.

"I really didn't mean that," she whispered.

Philipe raised her hair to brush his lips on the nape of her neck. "I did." His breath was hot on her flesh. "I love you."

Ruthana shrank away from him. Again she covered her face with her hands, but only for a moment. Looking up, she met his eyes and said, "I thought we were going over."

"I did, too." Philipe fumbled in the pocket

of his shirt for a cigarette. His hand with the lighter trembled when he lit it. "That was a bit too close."

"Much too close!"

"You mean the near accident, I suppose," Philipe said with a sardonic smile.

Ruthana had regained composure. "What else?" she asked.

CHAPTER 6

That night Ruthana told Penny, "Remember that ridge with a drop-off on either side of the road after you leave Saint Johns? Well, Philipe had started to say something when we'd reached the turn onto the ridge. There was that stupid goat, Clarence, eating grass in the middle of the road!"

"What was he going to say?" Penny asked.

Each girl was in pajamas, stretched on her own bed. Hugh had told them they would make an early start in the morning for Ladder Point on the west shore of Saba.

"I never found out," Ruthana said, "because the car skidded out of control when Philipe braked. We came so close to going over the edge I nearly had a heart attack."

"Wow!" Penny raised on an elbow. "Then what happened?"

"Why, nothing."

"You wouldn't lie a little, would you, Ruthana?"

"To you?" Ruthana was all innocence. "I don't think I could. You'd find me out."

"Oh, sure. Police and lawyers call on me instead of a lie-detector machine! Gullible should be my middle name instead of Marie. Sam's asked me to go to The Lido for the dance Saturday night. I hear they sell groceries at one end, and dance at the other. Did Philipe say anything to you?"

"No, he didn't."

Philipe had said very little after their narrow escape and impassioned kiss. She was getting used to the long silences when she was with him, but she wished he'd pushed his claim of loving her so they both could examine it.

I can't possibly love a man about whom I know so little, she thought. But her heart quickened when she remembered the expression on his face after he'd kissed her. Philipe had been as frightened as she was. Was it fear of her, or himself?

Penny patted a yawn. "I guess it's time for my beauty sleep. This mountain air gets to you." She laughed. "Saba isn't exactly my idea of what a Caribbean island would be like, but it grows on you."

"Good night," Ruthana said. "I think I'll take a bath."

In the tub Ruthana compared the way she was beginning to feel about Philipe, to the way she felt toward Hugh. She wondered how she could be so strongly attracted to both men. What did they have in common? Very little, Ruthana decided. Ruthana had always been careful about her feelings toward men, but here she was, about to fall in love with Philipe and Hugh at the same time!

"You're getting to be a mixed-up broad," Ruthana scoffed at herself.

It was a long time before she fell asleep.

When would she see Philipe again? He'd said

nothing. Tomorrow and the following days she and Penny would be working with Hugh. Perhaps Philipe wouldn't come again.

She'd nearly forgotten Katerina's portrait.

Hugh brought up the subject while eating an early breakfast with Ruthana and Penny the next morning.

"I hear you had quite a surprise yesterday at Philipe's," he said.

"Shock is a better word," Ruthana said. "I think I'm the victim of a really wild coincidence. There's no other rational explanation."

"I can think of one," Hugh said.

"Tell me."

"The pair of them want to sell you the painting for a fancy price," Hugh told her. "How much are they asking?"

"It isn't for sale," Ruthana told him. "Anyway, how could Celeste paint it without seeing me?"

"I don't know," Hugh admitted. "The whole thing, as Penny told it to me, sounds a little weird. Sam is usually a levelheaded guy, as I size him up, but he's ready to believe Celeste's yarn. The rest of the time we're here, I advise you to steer clear of the Simon brother-and-sister team."

"I doubt Ruthana is going to be able to manage that," Penny said, smiling. "If I'm any judge, Philipe has a thing for her, and wild horses couldn't keep him in Bottom."

Ruthana felt herself blush and was aware of Hugh's hard stare. "We're down here to work," he said. "You two are going to need all the rest you can get."

"Did I remember to tell you that Laidman has a slave-driver reputation?" Penny asked Ruthana. She turned to Hugh. "What mischief can a couple of girls get into on an island where it's lights out at eleven every night?"

"I can think of an answer to that, but I don't think I'll give it in mixed company," Hugh said, with a grin. "Come on, drink your coffee. Sam has horses rented and waiting for us over in Bottom."

"Horses!" Penny exclaimed. "I'm allergic to the darn animals! I sneeze, cry, and my nose runs."

"Then you'd better wear hiking boots," Hugh told her. "We have to climb over a small mountain to get to Ladder Point."

"I didn't bring hiking boots!" Penny wailed.

"I didn't, either," Ruthana said. "Just extra beach sandals."

"Oh, hell!" Hugh was disgusted. "I'll cancel the horses, and we'll buy two pairs of hiking boots. I brought mine."

"You were here before," Ruthana reminded Hugh. "We seldom need hiking boots on a modeling assignment. When was the last time you needed them?" she asked Penny.

"A year ago, up in the Adirondacks shooting ski stuff for Chapman," Penny said. "Each of us got a pair of ski boots out of that one, and Honey Caldwell broke her wrist. But it was okay. Chapman had finished shooting her."

"You'll take home hiking boots from this job," Hugh told them. "My treat because I didn't warn you."

"I want one of those straw hats," Penny said.

"Me, too," Ruthana agreed.

"They'll be your treat, and I'll take one," Hugh told them.

"I hope they're cheap," Penny said.

Hugh had rented a Volkswagen in Windwardside. They had discovered that hiking boots were very much in demand on Saba, and the local store had a good supply in women's sizes.

"All of us have a bit of mountain goat in our veins," the Saban storekeeper had told them. "This island only goes two ways, up and down."

Hiking from Bottom to Ladder Point, Hugh was loaded with tripods and cameras. Penny and Ruthana took turns carrying the picnic basket that Sable had packed. The climb up from Bottom, and down to Ladder Point, took them the better part of an hour. All three of them were winded when they reached the narrow, rocky beach being pounded by surf.

"I've convinced Madame Yvonne we should shoot her collection here on Saba," Hugh explained, "because her competitors will be using backgrounds on Bimini in the Bahamas or on Bermuda. Every splendid sweep of surf and sand looks like every other. Notice the texture and color of *these* rocks?"

It was a day with clear skies and a hot sun. In her hatbox, each girl had brought the styles that Hugh wanted to photograph that day. They used a shallow cave for a changing room.

They laughed when they discovered each girl had brought a small folding iron.

"Where did we think we were going to plug them in?" Ruthana asked.

"If there was an outlet in this cave, we wouldn't have electricity until five this afternoon," Penny said. "I feel as if we're on some kind of safari, with wild goats instead of elephants."

"We better get out there and go to work," Ruthana told Penny. "We have a restless white hunter."

Hugh was set up on the narrow beach.

He worked that day in black and white, as well as color, using polished metal sheets to eliminate face shadows, instead of flash bulbs. He used his Rolleiflex for action shots, when Penny and Ruthana played catch with a beach ball, but a portrait camera mounted on a tripod for posed photos.

Hugh worked faster than most of the photographers the girls knew, and they had to make fast changes to meet his pace.

Sable had packed thick ham-and-chicken sandwiches, made with the crusty bread she baked each morning, its delicious aroma drifting

94

through The Castle. There was Spanish wine, a Thermos of coffee, and a bottle of Saban dark rum. There were fresh limes to squeeze into the rum. The wine and rum Hugh chilled in the sea.

By the middle of the afternoon, clouds sailed the sky like fluffy white ships, and using red filters for his black and whites, Hugh got the cloud effects he wanted.

They finished working at four o'clock. "We won't be tackling those goat paths in the dark," Hugh had promised. He was good as his word.

Penny, Ruthana, and Hugh arrived back at The Castle in time for supper, tired but satisfied with their work.

"I seem to recognize that Volks with a rag top," Penny said when Hugh had parked his rented car behind it. "You've got company, Ruthana."

Ruthana's pulse quickened, but she said, "I doubt that. Philipe's probably making a business call to Sam."

They found Philipe with Sam and Arthur Teach in the bar off the dining patio. Sam's face was flushed and he was slightly drunk.

"Join us to lift an elbow," Sam invited Hugh,

Penny, and Ruthana. "Our honored guest, Saba's new administrator, is buying."

Philipe's dark eyes were for Ruthana. "I'd suggest a frosted rum fizz. Manuel here does the drink well."

Manuel was a slight, elderly man, his brown cheeks pitted with small scars, and Ruthana wondered if he was Sam's barkeeper who'd had a bottle of whiskey explode in his face.

"I'll have your rum fizz, please, Manuel," she said. "A bit light on the rum."

"Me, too, but don't hold the rum," Penny told Manuel. "We've had a long working day, with a hike thrown in."

"Make mine Scotch on the rocks with a water back," Hugh said.

Arthur was drinking Scotch and soda. "Hold the ice this time," he instructed Manuel. "Was it a good day?" he asked Hugh.

"The best," Hugh said.

Sam was drinking bourbon. He filled his highball glass from the bottle by his elbow. "Philipe's trying to persuade me to open another castle over in Bottom, sort of a cut-rate version of this one."

"That sounds like it might be a good idea,"

Hugh said in a neutral voice. "But why go cheap?"

"Most of our tourists are day-trippers who fly in from Saint Martin," Philipe explained. "A less expensive castle would encourage them to stay over a few days." He spoke as much to Ruthana as he did to Hugh. "It would make jobs here on Saba, and those we need."

"I can understand that, with so many men forced to leave the island to make a living," Ruthana said. "Your idea sounds like a good one," she told Philipe.

"Hell, what we've got here is a quiet little island that isn't flooded with tourists," Sam said. He raised his glass. "Here's to keeping it that way."

Hugh drank the toast. "Why change a working system?"

Philipe ignored the question. "I need to see you tonight," he said to Ruthana in a low voice. "Will you join me for supper?"

"Here?" she asked.

Philipe shook his head. "A place in Hell's Gate that I know."

"All right."

Philipe turned to the company. "Excuse us, please." He laid bills on the bar.

"Where are you going?" Hugh asked Ruthana.

Taking her elbow, Philipe whisked her into the patio.

"Out," she called back to Hugh, over her shoulder. "I need to freshen up, so I'll join you at the car," she told Philipe. "What should I wear?"

"Come as you are. A sweater and slacks is about as formal as we get on Saba," he told her. "Don't be too long."

Ruthana was breathless and wished Philipe had given her time to finish the rum fizz, but she said, "I won't be."

For the moment she was content to be swept along by Philipe. She sensed a jealous streak in Hugh, however, that she'd never expected.

Ruthana had always despised girls who enjoyed the attention of jealous admirers, and had encouraged their jealousy. Yet here she was between Hugh and Philipe, unsure of her own emotions, but at the same time, flattered. Maybe supper and an evening alone with Philipe would help her sort things out.

"You took awhile," Philipe said in an impatient voice when Ruthana joined him at the car.

"I needed to bathe and change," she explained. "I've had a long day of work."

Driving to Hell's Gate in the direction of the airport, Philipe had nothing to say. Ruthana watched his profile. From the way he drove, and his expression, she realized there was a ferment of reckless excitement within Philipe. She wondered where he might be taking her on this strange little island. And she remembered the fate of Katerina.

How had the Dutch girl felt toward her captor?

Philipe pulled up at the gate of a small brick cottage on the outskirts of the village. Behind the stone wall it looked like someone's home.

"Who lives here?" she asked Philipe.

"I do when I want to get away from my sister and Bottom," he told her frankly.

"Let me think about that a moment," Ruthana said. "I was assuming this place in Hell's Gate that you knew was a restaurant of some sort."

Philipe grinned. "Would you have come with me if you'd known we were coming here?"

"No."

"I didn't lie. This *is* a place I know here in Hell's Gate," Philipe said. "Are you afraid of me?"

"Yes."

"You speak frankly, Ruthana. I like that in a woman," Philipe told her. "Sam Lord would tell you that Philipe Simon is a man who keeps his word. If I give you mine that you'll come to no harm here, will you join me for the supper I've planned?"

"Yes, but on one condition," Ruthana said.

"And what would that condition be?"

"When I say it's time for you to take me back to The Castle, we leave." Ruthana laughed. "I've hiked far enough today."

"Agreed," Philipe said.

Inside, the cottage was one small room with a fireplace, bedroom, lavatory, and kitchen. There was no electricity. Candles were the only light. One wall of the bedroom, Ruthana noticed through the open door, was lined with books.

A cold supper was laid out on a table drawn

up to the fireplace. Two bottles of champagne were chilling in a silver ice bucket. The white tablecloth, Ruthana observed, was finest Irish linen; and the silverware gleaming in candlelight was of an antique pattern, obviously very old and probably worth a small fortune.

On the table were boiled shrimp on a mound of rice, sliced cold duck and chicken on a silver platter, a bowl of fresh red caviar, and hot rolls Philipe had brought from the kitchen. There was a watercress salad, Spanish olives, and radishes.

"Did you do all this?" Ruthana asked Philipe when they were seated at the table.

"No. I had a chef from the best restaurant on Saint Martin flown over this morning," Philipe admitted. "Are you properly impressed?"

"What girl wouldn't be, Philipe?"

His dark eyes twinkled. "Good. It was worth the expense."

"But rather extravagant, don't you think?" she asked. "What if I hadn't accepted your invitation?"

"I knew you would," Philipe told Ruthana. "You did return my kiss, you may remember."

Ruthana felt the color rising in her cheeks. "You didn't leave me much choice."

"With me you will always have a choice," Philipe assured Ruthana. "But let's discuss that later."

One of the now familiar silences fell between Philipe and Ruthana as they ate, warmed by the crackling fire in the fireplace. They sat across the table from each other. It was when they'd finished eating that Philipe refilled their champagne glasses for the third time.

Philipe raised his glass to Ruthana. "May you always be as glowingly beautiful as you are tonight."

"Thank you."

When he'd finished drinking his toast, Philipe smashed the glass on the hearth.

"Ruthana Franklin," he said, "I want you to be my mistress."

CHAPTER 7

Nothing of the emotional storm Philipe's remark had caused within Ruthana showed in her face as she finished her champagne. Carefully setting down her glass, she said, "Philipe, did I just hear you ask me to be your mistress?"

"Yes. Can I explain?" Philipe's face was blank, but his dark eyes smoldered. "I can't offer you marriage. For reasons you might understand if I could tell you them, I can never take a wife. But I want you, Ruthana, and there will never be anyone else. You have my sworn word about that."

Ruthana traced the rim of her empty champagne glass with a forefinger. "These reasons," she said, without meeting his eyes. "Would they have something to do with your sister?"

"Yes."

"You can't tell me what they are?"

"No."

"I want to believe that you're sincere," Ruthana said.

Philipe came around the table, and she rose to meet him. His hands cupped her shoulders, his eyes burned down into her face. Ruthana felt weak and robbed of her will. Philipe, she realized, was hypnotizing her, whether intentionally Ruthana couldn't say, but those eyes, and his grip on her shoulders, were draining all her strength and resistance.

She was acutely aware of the open bedroom door at her back, only a few quick steps away if Philipe should scoop her up in his arms. And should he do that, could she deny him her body?

"Ruthana." Philipe breathed her name as he pressed his cheek to hers. "Katerina." His hot breath brushed her ear. "Whoever you are, I love you and I always shall."

Ruthana went limp in his arms when Philipe's lips found hers. Then suddenly she was inflamed, and her arms circled his neck to crush his mouth to her own.

She heard him moan. Philipe bent and lifted her easily.

"No, Philipe." Her blood sang Yes! But Ruthana's head ruled. "Put me down, please."

Philipe set her on her feet. Ruthana turned away, to hide her face in her hands for a moment, then faced the man, her cheeks burning.

"Can we please go back to The Castle, Philipe?"

The man heaved a shuddering sigh and seemed to shake himself. "Immediately. Before I break my word," he said. "It's turned cold outside, you'll need a coat." He passed her to go into the bedroom and came back with a fleece-lined leather jacket. When Philipe had put it around her shoulders, he brushed a kiss on her cheek. "There."

"What was that for?" She asked.

"Because you haven't yet told me you won't

be my mistress," Philipe said. "I'm a very stubborn man, used to having my own way."

"We really don't know each other yet," Ruthana said. "How can you be so sure you want me?"

"Take my word for it," Philipe said. "You'll come to me all the way when you're ready, Ruthana. I accept that. I wouldn't want you any other way."

Silence rode between them back to The Castle. When they got there, Philipe caught Ruthana's hands. His face was stern and pale in the moonlight. "Did you enjoy our supper?" he asked.

"Very much."

"So you know how it can be with us here on Saba," Philipe said. "Good night, Ruthana." He dropped her hands to draw her toward him, kissing her forehead.

"Good night, Philipe, and thank you."

"For everything?" he asked.

"Yes," Ruthana said. "For everything."

Ruthana had to cross the patio to reach the stairway to the second floor of The Castle. It was long past eleven o'clock and dark except for a dappling of moonlight showing through the palms. She was halfway across the patio when Hugh spoke her name out of the darkness.

Startled, she looked around. Hugh came from the shadows, tossing a lock of hair from his forehead. "Where the hell have you been?"

"Out."

"You got off that smart remark before," Hugh accused. He peered closely at her uplifted face. "Simon is nothing but bad news for you, Ruthana. I told you to avoid him and his sister."

Ruthana's temper flared. "Hugh, for God's sake! So long as I do the work I came to Saba to do, what business is it of yours what I do or who I see? I'm a woman, not a silly girl. *So get off my back!*"

Hugh flinched from her outburst, but stood his ground. "I care too much to see you badly hurt," he told her. "I know Simon's type. You're just another conquest to him."

"Would you believe that I can take care of myself?" Ruthana asked. "How do you think I survived in New York before you came along, Hugh?"

"So I'm out of line," Hugh admitted. "Can I tell you something?"

"There's no way I can stop you," Ruthana said.

"Since that afternoon and evening at my place, I've been up the wall. 'You love her.' No, I don't. 'Yes, you do.' I wish to hell I could make up my mind! If you want me to be jealous, you've succeeded." Some of the tenseness went out of Hugh, and he smiled at her. "Hugh Laidman, invulnerable to any model's charm. Laidman, the perennial bachelor, proud as punch of his freedom!" He gently touched her chin with his hand. "Good night, slugger, and have sweet dreams."

Penny was awake when Ruthana reached their room. "Did you see Laidman?" she asked.

"Yes. He waylaid me in the patio. I got scolded about Philipe Simon. Laidman is acting like an irate parent and is beginning to remind me of Mother," Ruthana said, as much for her own benefit as Penny's. "Philipe and I had a quiet supper, and that was it."

Penny grinned. "That's the girl! Stick to that story. Did you ever hear the one about Goldilocks and the three bears? I used to enjoy that fairy tale."

"You're impossible!" Ruthana threw a pillow at her roommate.

Penny ducked and chortled. "Like Avis, I try harder, Ruthana." Then serious, she asked, "How is it with you and Philipe? Girl to girl. I've been getting some disturbing vibrations."

Ruthana perched on the edge of Penny's bed. "He wants to set me up as his mistress."

"Wow!" Penny gasped. "No wedding ring, bridal bouquet, and all that jazz?"

"None of that married scene," Ruthana confessed. "He has reasons that have to do with his sister. He won't say what they are. I don't know what to think, Penny."

Penny frowned and poked a finger at her cheek. "Do you think you can trust Philipe? I mean really trust him?"

"I wish I could answer that," Ruthana said, "but I can't."

"Living together isn't the no-no it used to be," Penny mused. "Honey Caldwell at our agency has a live-in boyfriend, and nobody minds, except maybe her parents up in Connecticut. They don't approve, as mine most certainly wouldn't! But they're not heavy about it with Honey. What am I trying to say? Here I sit—in the middle of the night yet!—and tell you something we both know. Why don't you tell me to shut my mouth?"

Ruthana gave Penny's tousled head a pat. "Go right along because I'm listening."

"Okay. What I'm trying to say is if it's right with Philipe and he really loves you as he should and isn't a roguish male out to conquer, why not? But you must be very sure, Ruthana. And would you listen to Penny Andrews, still a virgin at the advanced age of twenty-two, offering advice! Wow!"

"You talk a lot of good sense, Penny," Ruthana told her roommate. "I've heard every word that you've said. Thank you."

Penny yawned. "I've worn myself out offering advice. Good night."

Just as she was finally dropping off to sleep, Penny called Ruthana's name. "What is it now, Penny?" she asked in a sleep-thick voice.

"It's Laidman," Penny said.

Ruthana came wide awake and said, "What about him?"

"I've seen guys with cases on a girl, some pretty bad, too, but Laidman's for you is the near-fatal variety. It makes me jealous as heck, too! But keep him in the starting field, huh? I don't want to see a nice guy like Laidman left at the starting gate."

"You've got it, Penny, and made your point," Ruthana said. "Sleep well and dream beautiful, in color."

Penny giggled. "Sometime I'll tell you this full-color dream I keep having."

"Spare me tonight, okay?"

"You've got it."

Arthur Teach joined the three of them for an early breakfast. "I did some research last night on *Obeah*," he said. "It's a most fascinating subject! The most learned researchers can't agree where psychology gives way to supernatural powers."

"Tell us about it," Penny urged.

Hugh scowled. "I'd better check over my equipment before we start for Mount Scenery," he said, and left the table.

"At my prep school some of the boys thought it would be a lark to do their headmaster in, as it were." Arthur chuckled. "The first boy I met that morning asked me if I was feeling well. Actually it was close to the end of the term; I had a walking-tour vacation scheduled, and I was quite chipper. The next boy asked if I might be running a fever. So it went, all morning, and some of my teachers got in on the joke. By mid-afternoon I had a pounding headache and actually had a fever! My doctor, however, pronounced me fit as a fiddle."

"Wow!" Penny said. "What did you do to the rascals?"

"What could I? They were experimenting with applied psychology and, in the process, learned a good lesson. My point—and I do have one to make—is simply this. By wishing a person ill and letting him know it, a witch doctor can cause that person a great deal of mischief. Sam knows and may have told you his experience. So what is occult, and what is actual? Can we say the witch doctor, thrusting pins into a wax image of his victim and actually causing that person to feel pain where his image has been pierced, is an applied psychologist? I'm inclined to think so. But more learned men than I disagree."

Ponderous Sable waddled from the kitchen to refill their coffee cups.

112

"Where is Katche this morning?" Ruthana asked.

"She be hexed," Sable said. "Someone wish her bad. She go to Saint Martin for *gris-gris* and come back before that someone break rotten egg on the shore. Katche be all right."

"A case in point," Arthur said when Sable had returned to the kitchen. "If you want a visitor to stay on Saba, you place a black cat under a tub. If you kill that cat, accidentally or otherwise, you have to live out its nine lives. The third night after a funeral is the most dangerous. *Jumbies* will surely get into your house unless you've taken the proper precautions. This little island is riddled with such beliefs, black and white people alike subscribing to them."

"What about zombies?" Penny asked.

"Are you two coming?" Hugh called into the patio. "We're wasting time."

"Zombies will be the subject of my next lecture," Arthur said with a grin and wink.

"You've promised," Penny told him. On their way to join Hugh, she asked Ruthana, "What do you think about *Obeah*? That picture of you Celeste painted has me beginning to believe in this reincarnation bit."

113

"Let's say that I'm a skeptic," Ruthana said.

"You do have Dutch ancestors, Ruthana."

"So do at least half the people in Pennsylvania. You know that. I bet you'd find some on your family tree if you dug around the roots."

"My maiden aunt, Eulalie, makes the genealogical scene in our family," Penny told Ruthana, laughing. "The poor thing spends half her time in the library, and she even went to Washington once. They have a genealogy club where she lives."

"Where is that?" Ruthana asked.

"Bristol. Do you know it?"

"Yes. My mother's sister, Aunt Rebecca, lives there. Mrs. Thomas Talbot. She and Mother have been on cool terms ever since Aunt Rebecca discovered a villain in The Whiskey Rebellion on our family tree."

Penny laughed. "Daddy's people came over as indentured servants, and he's proud of it."

"Father's family was Quaker and knew William Penn. Coming from Philadelphia, we're related to Benjamin Franklin, of course. Mother makes a point of bringing him up on just about every social occasion."

"Why shouldn't she?" Penny asked. "I'd do it."

Ruthana laughed. "Which reminds me—I've just brought up Ben Franklin, haven't I?"

"And William Penn," Penny pointed out. "Don't be too crass with your mother."

"I know I shouldn't be," Ruthana admitted. "She's the only one I have. I'd better write her tonight."

Hugh had located a four-wheel-drive Land-Rover in Windwardside, and they reached Mount Scenery in that vehicle. Thick clouds and threatening rain shrouded the volcano's peak. Hugh wanted to use the mountain slopes for background. He had another reason for wanting clear shots of the mountain and told Ruthana about it.

"Your friend Simon called early this morning," Hugh said.

"What did he want?" Ruthana asked.

"He's commissioned me to make a series of photographs showing Saba's rugged, scenic beauty for some kind of tourist brochure he'll have printed. I'm to put him in touch with a

115

good advertising agency when we get back to New York."

"That sounds good," she told him.

Hugh shrugged. "I don't know. Maybe he's just trying to buy me off. I wouldn't be too surprised."

The three of them poked around Mount Scenery the rest of the morning, waiting for the cloud cover to dissolve, but while they were eating their picnic lunch at noon, the clouds congealed and torrents of rain came down.

"We can't do any good today," Hugh decided. "We'll rove on back to The Castle. I suppose we could play a few hands of bridge, if we could dig up a fourth."

"Sam Lord?" Penny suggested.

Hugh shook his head. "Sam's game is high-stake poker. I was thinking of Arthur Teach, if we can keep him away from spook stories."

"I like his stories," Penny said. "Zombies are his next lecture subject."

"Oh, Lord!" Hugh said.

When they got back to The Castle, it was to find Arthur Teach had gone for the day to Bottom. Hugh invited Ruthana to the Saturday night dance at The Lido, but was out of the mood for a three-hand game of hearts.

It was Saturday afternoon, and with rain pouring down outside, Hugh decided he'd take a nap. "I want to be at my best for Saba night-life," he told the girls. "A fellow at my advanced age of twenty-eight can't get too much sleep."

"Shall I bring you a hot rum toddy with a licorice stick, Grandfather?" Penny asked.

Ruthana laughed. "More likely a hot-water bottle for his cold feet."

"Show your boss proper respect, girls," Hugh said. "And let me think about that last remark you made, Ruthana. Was it a Freudian slip?"

Ruthana blushed. "Nothing like that, Laidman."

The rain was chilling Saba. In the bar Manuel mixed Penny and Ruthana hot rum toddies, and they settled down to a game of double solitaire. Sam Lord drifted in. He'd just returned from the airport with a party of guests arriving for the New Year's Eve celebration on Monday.

"It's liable to be a pretty wild wingding," he warned the girls, sitting at their table to kibitz the solitaire game while nursing a rum punch. "Red king on your black queen, Penny."

"Shut up, Sam."

"I've served with these four guys in wars here and there," Sam said. "Stop cheating, Ruthana."

"Shut up, Sam."

"We try to get together somewhere every New Year's Eve," Sam told them. Reaching to move one of Penny's cards, Sam had his hand slapped. "Ouch! As I haven't said yet, Laidman and you two are invited to our bash. It's all right, because the fellows brought their own girls. Just stay out of dark corners as the wassail flows. We're still dated for The Lido?" he asked Penny.

"We are unless you stand me up," she said.

"No chance of that," Sam told her.

"I'll be going with Hugh," Ruthana told him.

"It's been a lot of years since I've doubledated," Sam said. "More than I like to remember."

CHAPTER 8

By Saturday evening the pouring rain had slowed to a drizzle, with the cloud cover over Saba beginning to thin and a new moon occasionally peeking down at the small Caribbean island. The smell of freshly-ground coffee drifted from the grocery-store end of the long room, and the pounding jukebox set up a vibration the guests could feel through the soles of their shoes.

Saba's unmarried girls clustered in front of the grocery counter, clutching black shawls around their shoulders and chattering like excited magpies, while their swains huddled around the throbbing jukebox, joking and laughing.

"What you now see is the ancient courting rites of the young male and female Sabans," Sam announced. "From these Saturday night festivities, future generations of Saban youngsters are born, if you can believe it."

"Now that's interesting," Ruthana said. "The only thing is how do they manage that with all the boys up here and the girls down there?"

"She has a point," Penny told Sam. The four of them shared one of the few tables surrounding the dance floor. "I've always understood a certain degree of close proximity is necessary to make babies. Of course, things may be different here on Saba, but just the same, the boys here and the girls over there is food for thought."

"Have you told her yet how trees manage?" Hugh asked Ruthana. "And the flowers?"

"I haven't gone into any detail," Ruthana said. "You see, Penny, there are these bees. . . ."

"What does making honey have to do with tree and flower babies?" Penny asked.

Sam stood up and said, "Dance, Penny? I'll whisper all about it into your shell-like ear."

"I've never danced to the Nashville sound," Penny told him. "It should be fun."

"We're finally alone together." Hugh had to raise his voice over the wail of a country singer. Reaching across the table, he took Ruthana's hands. "Ever since you sorted out my cupboards, I've wanted to tell you. . . ."

Ruthana lost the trend of his conversation as the Nashville singer cried his lament, and she asked, "What?"

"*I love you!*"

Hugh's words echoed in the sudden silence. Every face in The Lido turned their way. Red to his ears, Hugh crossed to the jukebox, dropped in a coin, and punched up a waltz.

Ruthana rose to meet him, and they waltzed away from the table. Saban young men and young women now were dancing. Sam waltzed Penny with a flourish. She was laughing at something Sam had just said.

"I didn't mean to make that a 'Hear-this!' deal," Hugh said. "Anyway, now you know what's been bugging me."

"Thank you," Ruthana murmured.

"You're welcome." Hugh kissed her forehead. His arms tightened and drew her slender body closer. "What can we do about it?" he whispered.

"I don't know yet," she confessed.

With Hugh's breath in her hair and his arms holding her close, Ruthana felt warm and safe, and Philipe seemed far away, part of another life. Yet Ruthana knew he would be back to stir her blood.

"I really don't know, Hugh," she whispered, "but I thank you again for loving me."

"Can we discuss it?" he asked.

"Not now, please."

"Okay." The waltz was over. Hugh gave her a brotherly kiss. "You say when."

Back at the table they found Sam and Penny busy with their own conversation.

"Only my daddy can waltz better than you," Penny was telling Sam. "That's a compliment, because he and Mother used to win trophies for their waltzing. It's a lost art."

"Only we old men keep it alive," Sam said in a wry voice.

"You're not old, Sam. Just mature. Dry behind the ears." Penny smiled. "The years look good on you, my friend."

"Can I borrow your date for the next waltz?" Ruthana asked Penny. "It's a fair exchange. Laidman is a master also."

"These wenches are buttering us good," Sam told Hugh. "Maybe we should buy them a drink."

"Good idea," Hugh agreed. "Ply them with liquor. 'Candy is dandy but liquor is quicker,' according to Ogden Nash."

"And 'Men never make passes at girls who wear glasses,'" Ruthana said. "Neither Penny nor I are myopic, but I just thought I'd throw that in."

"I need reading glasses to look up numbers in the telephone book," Penny said. "Does that make me safe, Ruthana?"

"It all depends on what number you call," Ruthana said.

"I'll pop for the first round, Hugh," Sam said. "All this sparkling wit has me dizzy."

Too soon it was eleven o'clock and generator shutdown time. The sky had cleared, and the sliver of a moon rode high. Sam and Penny walked to The Castle ahead of Hugh and Ruthana, Sam's arm around Penny's waist, her head against his shoulder.

Hugh and Ruthana walked with linked hands. "A Saturday night on Saba at The Lido has its points," Hugh told Ruthana. "We must do this again sometime."

"I was afraid you wouldn't ask me," she said.

"Modest women are hard to find in this day and age." Hugh smiled at her. "I'd like to put a lock on this one and throw away the key."

"Be patient with me, Hugh," Ruthana said. "Right now I'm a mixed-up woman."

Hugh kissed her hair. "You'll get your head straight."

"It's my heart that worries me," Ruthana told him.

Over rum nightcaps on the patio, Sam announced, "The New Year's Eve party will be a masquerade. No one unmasks until midnight. Do I hear any objections?"

"From me you don't," Ruthana said. "I've never been to a masquerade."

"It will really be a fun thing, Sam," Penny told him. "But what do I wear?"

"Come as Eve," Sam suggested.

"Can't," Penny said.

"Why not?" Hugh asked.

"Mother would spank me if she found out. I know, Ruthana. We dress as twins with chignons so our hair doesn't give us away."

"That's a super idea," Ruthana agreed.

"You won't be the only twins," Sam said. "I've invited the Simons."

When the women said good night and went to their room, Ruthana failed to see how she could avoid a discussion of Hugh's too public protestation of love, but she needn't have worried. Penny was filled to the brim with Sam Lord.

"I've always tended to groove to older men," Penny confessed. "And maybe I ought to see a shrink, but callow youth in a male bores me. Sam's been around, and around again, but the guy is just plain sweet. Do you know what he did?"

"Not until you tell me, Penny."

"He *asked* if he might kiss me! Asked! Can you imagine? I didn't know what to say, so I kissed him, and got trembly."

"And then?" Ruthana prompted.

"We were outside, in the street, and Clarence picked that moment to munch a tin can or something. Sam threw a rock at him. I thought I'd have to kiss Sam again, but I didn't."

"Isn't he old enough to be your father?" Ruthana asked.

"Someone always comes up with that chestnut," Penny said, "and I hate it! Old men are old. Sam isn't an old man! He's everything a mature man ought to be, and he's never been married."

"And you want to snare him?" Ruthana asked.

Penny's eyes sparkled. "I'm going to, so just watch me."

"That look on your face tells me that you probably will," Ruthana said. "What if he wants a mistress, though, instead of a loving wife?"

"That bridge I'll cross when—and if—I ever come to it," Penny told her. "Right now I want him and a ring on my finger, but I've been known to compromise—however, not very often. We Andrewses are a stubborn breed."

"I wish you all the luck you need," Ruthana told her roommate.

"Daddy says people make their own luck," Penny replied. "But thank you anyway."

* * *

Ruthana found that she cherished Hugh's blurted *"I love you!"* But in bed alone she found Philipe Simon was very much back in her thoughts and coursing through her blood. She wondered what he'd say to her Monday night and thought about his puzzling relationship with Celeste. Incest was out of the question! Did he fear Negro genes in his blood? He needn't, so far as she was concerned, but if it was a factor, and came up, they could adopt.

Or was that a solution? Ruthana found she wanted children of her own, and Hugh could certainly give them to her. Hugh. She remembered how close to him he'd held her when they'd danced, the way the corners of his eyes crinkled when he grinned, and she found that Hugh and Philipe were double images, like two on the same negative.

"Ruthana?"

"I'm asleep, Penny."

"I told Sam when I marry it will be in white," Penny said. "Do you know what he said about that?"

"What?"

Penny sighed. "Sam said a bride in white was the only kind he wanted."

127

"That almost sounds like a proposal, Penny."

"There was a qualifying clause tacked on," Penny told her sadly. "Sam added *if* he ever married."

Their clumsy, square-toed hiking boots gave Penny and Ruthana the idea for their costume. "We can go as twin Charlie Chaplins," Ruthana said. "We've both a pair of black slacks."

"What about shirts?" Penny asked.

"You borrow from Sam, and I'll tap Hugh."

"Great! I saw canes where we bought our boots. Secondhand clothes, too. We can get our coats there, but what do we do about derbies? Men don't seem to wear them here on Saba."

"Do you suppose Sam would send to Saint Martin for us?" Ruthana asked. "A lot of British tourists go there during the winter."

"Sure, Sam will get them for us," Penny said with confidence. "He wants to take me shopping there before we go back to New York. It's a free port, you know. All kinds of real bargains. I only wish that I'd brought more money."

"I can lend you some," Ruthana volunteered.

"Thanks, but no thanks," Penny said. "I have

some credit cards if they'll take them. I'll have to ask Sam."

"What do we do about masks?" Ruthana asked.

"Get some paper and make them," Penny said. "I don't want a mustache painted on my upper lip, just in case."

Ruthana laughed. "Me, neither, come to think. Can you draw? I can't."

"I'm good at it," Penny bragged. "How do you suppose Sam will come?"

"I don't know. Why don't you ask him?"

"I did, but he wouldn't say," Penny admitted. "Sam wants to surprise me."

"Men can be full of surprises," Ruthana said, "and there's a cliché if I ever heard one."

"My mother says wives should be, even after they've been married donkey's years."

"I think I'd like your mother," Ruthana told Penny and sighed. "I love mine, but I wish I could like her, too."

"I'll share my mother with you," Penny said.

"Thanks, Penny, but no thanks." Ruthana smiled. "I've just made a New Year's resolution. I'm going to *like* my mother next year, whatever she says or does. I've acted like a spoiled brat,

I'm afraid. Mother and I are two adult women now. It's time we knew it and went on from there."

"Good resolution," Penny said. "My mother would approve. She has always treated me as another adult, even when I was having teen-age tantrums. But do you know what she did once, when I sneaked out of the house to meet a boy?"

"Locked you in?" Ruthana asked.

"No. She *spanked* me! I was sixteen, too. Wow! How humiliated can you get?"

"I'll bet that cured your sneaky streak."

"It really turned me around. She used Daddy's work belt. I couldn't sit properly for days."

"My mother used to lock me in a closet, until she read somewhere that would make me afraid of the dark. After that I stood in corners. I liked the closet drill better. In there I could scold my mother for being so mean."

Penny laughed. "I'll bet you told her a thing or two."

Ruthana laughed with her. "I sure did. I gave her back every scolding she'd given me that I could remember. If I'm not mother's little lady, you're not Ruthana's big lady, I used to say, and like that."

"We'll need neckties," Penny said. "The Little Tramp always wore one. Did you ever go to that theater in New York that shows old movies? It's a real thrill. One of my ex-boyfriends used to take me."

"Ex?" Ruthana asked.

"That's right," Penny said. "All three are ex, now that I've met Sam."

"You do burn your bridges, don't you?" Ruthana said. "I admire that."

"Yes, but it could leave me stranded. Have you ever thought of that?" Penny asked.

"It occurs to me," Ruthana said. "Real long neckties?"

"Right." Penny showed Ruthana with her hands.

"Narrow ties?" Ruthana asked.

"Right. Sam can get them for us," Penny said.

Ruthana wished and prayed that Penny's newfound faith in Sam Lord wouldn't be betrayed, and envied the other girl's single-minded devotion to one man. She was finding it disturbing to have her own loyalties divided between Philipe and Hugh.

Sam Lord's *compadres*, on Saba only New Year's Eve (they and their girl friends would be flying back to Miami Beach New Year's Day), were Sid Ford, an Australian soldier-of-fortune; Johnny Bolanski, a Polish refugee; Red Farber and Bill Britten, both Americans, both pilots. Farber and Britten carried the scars of imprisonment on the Isle of Pines, after the Bay of Pigs fiasco. Both of these men, Ruthana suspected, were C.I.A. operatives.

Bolanski had broken through the Iron Curtain in a stolen truck, killing two border guards in West Germany on his way to freedom. He was a slow-moving and slow-spoken giant of a man, six foot seven, with the build of a wrestler or weight lifter.

Johnny Bolanski's girl was Nancy. She was a slender little redhead, about half Johnny's size. Aussie Sid Ford had brought Mabel to Saba.

Mabel was a long-stemmed, willowy blonde from a Miami Beach chorus line, and effected a southern drawl that Penny swore she could cut with a knife.

"I'll bet Miami Beach is the only place she's been below the Mason-Dixon line," Penny told Ruthana.

"You haven't got a taker here," Ruthana said. "I doubt she can whistle Dixie and probably thinks the Stars and Bars is a chain of cocktail lounges."

"We really shouldn't be so catty," Penny decided.

"To make up for it," Ruthana told Penny, "we'll be especially nice to Sid Ford's date."

Red Farber and Bill Britten had brought two Cuban girls, petite sisters, Lupe and Inez. The Cuban girls shared a room, as did Farber and Britten, and for Lupe and Inez it would be a very proper weekend.

Sam had warned his friends it would be a masquerade party, so they'd brought costumes for their dates and themselves.

Ruthana and Penny quickly sensed a quiet desperation in all of these men. They always ate, drank, and moved around in a tight group, as if always alert and ready to repel an attack.

"I just can't imagine Sam ever being like them," Penny confided to Ruthana. "I've seldom known more polite guys, but they scare the bejesus out of me!"

Sam Lord's New Year's Eve masquerade parties were a legend and institution on Saba. As well as Philipe and Celeste Simon, everyone who was anyone on Saba had been invited. Two bartenders had been flown down from Saint Martin to assist Manuel, and a hotel chef from there took over Sable's kitchen. She would sulk and pout until he flew back to Saint Martin.

CHAPTER 9

Sam managed two Charlie Chaplin outfits for Ruthana and Penny, complete with baggy pants, tight-fitting coats, shirts, neckties, and clumsy shoes. There were masks, too, and derby hats.

"Wow! How in the world did you manage, Sam?" Penny asked.

Sam grinned. "I know a few wizards."

"Come on, Sam!" Ruthana said. She'd been examining the costumes and had found a label. "You had these flown down from a costume-rental place in Miami Beach, didn't you?"

"Guilty," Sam admitted.

Hugh had borrowed a wet suit from the store in Windwardside stocking scuba diving equipment. Sid Ford and Red Farber would come as Mississippi riverboat gamblers. Bolanski had brought down a Frankenstein monster outfit, suitably enough. Bill Britten would be a Western gunslick, complete with pearl-handled six-shooters, weapons that not only looked real, but were genuine.

"Bill has probably one of the best weapon collections in the world," Sam told Hugh, Penny, and Ruthana. "You name it, he has it in his Saint Petersburg place. And he's expert with every weapon he owns. Wherever there's a small war or revolution, one side or the other sends for Britten."

The Four Musketeers, as Sam called them, would soon be off for Rhodesia. "But don't spread that around," he cautioned Hugh, Ruthana, and Penny. Hugh had offered to take pictures at the party. "It's okay to shoot the boys in costume and masks, but don't snap any of them unmasked," Sam cautioned. "They're a bit touchy about having their pictures taken."

"Why is that, Sam?" Penny asked.

"You make lethal enemies fighting these small wars," Sam explained. "Losers hunt down those most responsible for them losing. A snapshot helps a hunter identify his prey." Over afternoon cocktails on the patio Sam was in an expansive mood. "Haven't you wondered why I chose Saba when I retired?"

"I understand now," Hugh said. "You can keep track of who comes and goes. Right?"

"Partly that," Sam said. "Just as important, I know just about everyone on the island, and they know me. A fellow sailing around the Caribbean alone came ashore at Ladder Point last year. He'd hijacked the boat to run marijuana and was tiptoe enough to make some of my friends on Saba suspicious. I had the word he was around ten minutes after he hit the beach. An hour later he was checked-out."

"Do they grow marijuana here?" Ruthana asked.

"No. The Mary Jane smuggler was having boat trouble," Sam said. "De Graaf put him on the next plane out and kept the boat for the owners to come down and collect."

"The guy picked the wrong island that time," Hugh said.

137

Sam nodded. "The point is, here on Saba I'm safe. Well, as safe as I'd be anywhere," Sam confessed. "I still sleep with a forty-five under my pillow."

There was a strained expression on Penny's face, Ruthana noticed, as she listened to Sam's recital.

"Two people can keep a sharper lookout than one, Sam," she said gamely.

Sam finished his drink with a thoughtful expression on his face.

The chef from Saint Martin served a roasted suckling pig with an apple in its mouth for New Year's Eve supper in the patio. Philipe and Celeste were the only outside guests invited to The Castle for that meal.

Arthur Teach had flown off to meet a nephew, a petroleum engineer visiting on Curaçao, doing a survey for the Royal Dutch Shell Company.

"I'll be sorry to miss the festive occasion here," he'd told Sam, "but at my age, maybe it's just as well."

Philipe and Celeste had brought their costumes and had taken rooms at The Castle for the night.

Philipe treated Ruthana with studied formality at supper, as if there was nothing between them, but whether that was for the benefit of Celeste, or the rest of the company, she couldn't be sure.

One thing Ruthana quickly realized was that Celeste's dark eyes were always following her. There was something almost malevolent in the woman's gaze. It gave Ruthana a prickling feeling, and she felt a hollowness in the pit of her stomach.

Ruthana was seated between Philipe and Hugh, and Sam sat between Celeste and Penny. No one was in costume yet. The Four Musketeers, and their dates, shared a table in the corner of the patio.

Anticipation of a party, Ruthana decided, was almost as exciting as the party that night would be. The main bar would be here at The Castle, but there would be a service bar at The Lido for dancers. Sam had rented that place for the night in order to accommodate all his guests. Earlier that day Penny and Ruthana had helped with the decorations.

Cocktails made from Sam's best Château Lafite champagne were served at supper. "I'll bet

139

this bubbly cost Sam thirty-five or forty dollars a bottle," Hugh whispered to Ruthana.

Sam overheard. "Fifty-five," he told Hugh around the back of his hand, "but, what the hell? New Year's only comes around once a year."

To play for dancers at The Lido, Sam had had a five-piece steel band, the most popular group in Kingston, flown down from Jamaica.

Celeste, Ruthana noticed, toyed with her food. Around her neck tonight she wore a gold medallion that was identical to Philipe's.

"May I have a close look at that?" Ruthana asked Philipe, pointing to his gold medallion.

"Surely." He ducked out of the gold link chain and handed it to her.

The medallion was a little larger than a silver dollar. It was round, with arcane words inscribed around the rim, four pentagrams within the circle, and a square tipped on end in the center. Philipe, with a smile, studied Ruthana's profile as she turned the heavy gold in her hand to inspect it.

Hugh was as interested as she was. "It represents the wizard's magic circle, doesn't it?"

Hugh asked Philipe when Ruthana had handed him the medallion. "In reality a nine-foot circle?"

"I see you have some knowledge of the arcane," Philipe told Hugh. "Each pentagram represents a direction, with north at the top where it's linked to the chain."

Hugh nodded, still studying the medallion closely. "What's the procedure when the wizard, or whatever you want to call him, enters the circle?"

"He doesn't enter it," Philipe said. "He draws it around him on the ground or floor. The circle is his only protection from whatever spirits he calls up."

"I see," Hugh said.

"I, who am the servant of the all highest, do by virtue of His Holy Name Immanuel, sanctify unto myself the circumference of nine feet around me," Philipe intoned in a low voice. "That's the opening drill, before he summons anyone. Next, he calls on *Glaurah* from the east, *Garron* from the west, *Cabon* from the north, and *Berith* from the south. Now he can call up the demons."

Hugh handed the medallion back to Philipe. "The Old Religion."

"Yes," Philipe agreed. "It has much more in common with Christianity than we're willing to admit. I mean the forms of the Old Religion," Philipe explained. "Wizard or magician, he's the priest. The magic circle, his altar and church. Incense is burned within its confines."

Ruthana knew little of the arcane and occult, these subjects not being taught at smart boarding and finishing schools, and her religious beliefs inclined toward Quakerism. What Philipe was telling her and Hugh lifted the corner of a curtain beyond which she'd resolved never to venture. A good girl friend at the last school she'd attended disappeared into the maw of some esoteric Oriental cult, only to be rescued by her parents when she was on the brink of a complete nervous breakdown.

So what Philipe and Hugh were discussing disturbed and frightened her.

With a slight frown on her face Celeste watched Ruthana from across the table, fingering the medallion at her throat. She didn't hear Sam ask if she wanted another champagne cocktail. Ruthana met Celeste's eyes, unwillingly, but then couldn't look away. She felt again as if her own will was being drained away, much as she'd felt with Philipe the other night.

"Damn the woman!" Involuntarily she whispered the thought.

"Excuse me," Hugh said. "What did you say?"

His voice broke the spell. "Nothing important," she said. "Too much champagne. It has me talking to myself."

"It's only worrisome when yourself starts talking back, Ruthana." Philipe grinned and patted the hand she'd rested on the edge of the table.

Celeste is gloating now, Ruthana thought. *Whatever kind of crazy contest we're having, she just won the first round.*

By eight o'clock the New Year's Eve party at The Lido, and The Castle, was in full swing. Saban youngsters had been enlisted to chauffeur rented Volkswagens and shuttle guests back and forth. Philipe had arranged for the generator to run all night and into the early morning hours.

Sam Lord as the host, Ruthana noticed, was watching his drinks tonight. Her costume and Penny's drew favorable comment from everyone, although they soon got rid of their shoes and danced barefooted. Philipe danced with nearly professional skill and easily won the limbo contest for men.

Mabel and Nancy did a song-and-dance act at The Castle and had to repeat it down at The Lido. Lupe and Inez sang Cuban ballads. They, too, had to put on two performances.

The Jamaican steel band, inspired by Saban dark rum served them in pitchers, beat out frenzied Caribbean rhythms, with sad and sweet measures as a change of pace. Listening to these, Ruthana found herself on the brink of tears more than once, although she couldn't understand a word of the lyrics.

There was calypso.

Through the evening Hugh and Philipe shared her, and it was a heady experience to dance in one man's arms, and then the other's.

Sam, when he wasn't seeing to his guests, took nearly all of Penny's dances. She was radiant, and prettier than Ruthana had ever seen her. It was obvious to everyone that Penny Andrews was totally in love.

Ruthana lost track of Celeste.

Johnny Bolanski did a surprisingly graceful cossack's dance as the evening wore on toward the new year. Sid Ford, in a good baritone, sang Australian bush ballads. Red Farber managed to juggle five whiskey shot-glasses, after he'd emptied them single-handed and drew a round of applause.

Ruthana soon lost track of all the Sabans who introduced themselves to her or were introduced by Philipe. Once she asked him, "What's become of your sister?"

Philipe shrugged his shoulders. "Am I her keeper?" he asked. He seemed indifferent. "I could use a breath of air." They'd just returned to The Lido from The Castle, and Hugh wasn't with them. "Let's go see if God still has the stars pinned up there."

They stepped out into Windwardside's main street, Philipe holding Ruthana's hand. It was a warm night of brilliant stars.

Clarènce clumped down the street past The Lido. "Does that goat ever sleep?" Ruthana asked Philipe.

Philipe scratched his head. "Now that you mention it, I don't think so. Some Sabans consider him someone's Familiar."

"What's a Familiar?" Ruthana asked.

They were walking down the street, toward

the sheer cliff that rose out of the sea. "Witches are supposed to have a familiar demon, in the form of a black cat, a dog, or perhaps a goat like Clarence. It follows her wherever she goes." Philipe's hand, holding Ruthana's, was warm. "The Familiar is a sort of mascot. No self-respecting witch would ever be without one."

They'd come to the brink of the cliff. Down below, hundreds of feet, surf was beating at the rocky base of the cliff. The night muted the sound of it. There was no fence or any other barrier on the lip of the cliff.

"Does anyone ever fall off here?" Ruthana asked Philipe.

"Not lately," he said. "Everyone on Saba knows enough not to fall off a cliff. The French once tried to capture Saba by scaling a cliff like this one. Sabans rolled rocks down on top of them. That soon changed their minds, and they went away."

Philipe's arm was warm around Ruthana's waist as they stared at the sea and surf pearling along the foot of the cliff. Ruthana felt as if they stood at the edge of the world, looking off into infinity. She decided Hugh was probably looking for them by this time, but wanted to stay here beside Philipe for a few more minutes.

"Stay here on Saba, Ruthana." Philipe's low voice was compelling. "We could have so much if we were together. I fell in love with Celeste's painting before we met in San Juan. Can we argue with fate?"

Ruthana slipped from the circle of his arm. "I don't believe in fate, Philipe. I want to control my own life and emotions. Unless my head rules my heart, I'm lost!"

Philipe placed a gentle hand over her heart. "I can feel what it's saying," he whispered. "Philipe, Philipe, Philipe."

Ruthana pressed his hand to her breast for a moment and felt its warmth through her costume shirt, then guided it down to his side. She faced him with an upturned face, and stars swam in her eyes.

When he leaned to kiss her mouth, Ruthana touched a restraining finger to his lips. "Please, no."

It was Ruthana's head speaking. Her heart was saying something else.

A foot crunched gravel, and they both turned to face Hugh. His face in the moonless darkness was a pale oval, with dark smudges for eyes. "Nice night," Hugh said in a controlled, neutral voice. "Ten until midnight. Sam asked about you two, so I came looking."

Both Philipe and Ruthana knew it was a lie.

"My host!" Philipe muttered.

Ruthana between them, Philipe and Hugh started back toward The Lido. "Actually, I'm a liar, and you two know it," Hugh said. "Sam didn't send me."

Hugh held Ruthana's right hand, Philipe her left.

"Laidman, I'd like very much to hate your guts," Philipe said across Ruthana in a pleasant voice. "You don't give me an excuse, however. I wish you would."

"Sorry about that, Simon," Hugh said. "I have to return the compliment."

Ruthana was suddenly angry with both men. She jerked away from them, to stumble toward The Lido, tears stinging her eyes. Philipe and Hugh let her go.

Just inside the door Ruthana bumped an embracing couple apart and found herself facing Penny and Sam. Without a word, or flicker of expression, Sam reached for his handkerchief and handed it to Ruthana.

"Ruthana!" Penny was distressed. "Whatever in the world?"

Behind her Ruthana heard Sam say, "Leave her alone, Penny."

On the dance floor they were counting down to the new year. "Now!" someone cried.

Bill Britten drew his pearl-handled six-shooters and squeezed the triggers. He didn't stop pulling until he'd fired all six blanks in each gun and the light bulbs closest to him shattered, glass tinkling to the dance floor.

Ruthana collapsed in a chair, buried her face on her knees for a moment, and then was laughing hysterically, shoulders shaking.

Sam and Penny found her. Sam pulled Ruthana up out of the chair, snatched her off her feet, swung her through three complete circles, then kissed her soundly. "Happy new year!"

Penny grabbed Ruthana's hands when Sam had set her back on her feet. Eyes sparkling, Penny said, "You're the first to know."

"Know what?" Ruthana was calm and limp now.

"Sam and I. We're going to be married!"

* * *

There was a thin line of light along the eastern horizon when Sam and Penny with Hugh and Ruthana were in the patio for a final drink.

"Sort of a daycap," Penny said.

Behind the bar Sam mixed eggs, orange juice, and gin, pouring their drinks into tall, frosted glasses. All the guests were in bed or had gone home.

Hugh proposed the toast. "May the four of us travel with the wind at our backs and be in heaven before the devil knows we're dead."

Sam grinned happily. "I'll drink to that."

Ruthana thought he looked ten years younger. When she'd finished her drink, Hugh took the glass and kissed her lips. "Happy new year."

"The same to you," Ruthana said.

CHAPTER 10

New Year's morning, Ruthana was the first one down for breakfast. Katche was back from wherever she'd been, and Sable was beaming now that she had her kitchen to herself once again. Ruthana had her melon, bacon and eggs, and coffee at a kitchen table with the two women.

"Those party last night go fine?" Sable wanted to know.

"It was very good, Sable," Ruthana said. "I

think everyone had a good time. How did you and Katche celebrate the new year?"

"My man came home yesterday," Katche said. "We made a baby."

Ruthana noticed the *gris-gris* nestled in the soft hollow of the girl's throat. Katche fingered it. "Someone on Saba hexed me about a baby," she said, "but now it will come. You'll see."

Sable patted the girl's shoulder. "This one a good young woman." Sable was obviously proud of Katche. "Strong babies will come to her and her man now. I tell her where to go, what man to see. Katche do what I say. Brave young woman, this one."

"You and your man will have a wonderful family," Ruthana said. Somehow she felt sure that they would. "And how did you celebrate?" she asked Sable.

"Go to Bottom. Limbo dance go on there all night." Sable grinned. "Found me a limbo man."

Arthur Teach had come back from Curaçao on the morning flight. He joined them in the kitchen for his coffee, lacing it with rum. "I see that you survived the festive evening," he told Ruthana. "It must have been quite a bash. Sam always does New Year's Eve up brown."

"It was fun," she said. "Do you know, that's the first New Year's Eve party I've ever attended. I've been invited to parties before, but something always came up."

"Now that you're baptized in Sam's wassail bowl, you'll come back another New Year's," Arthur said. "In Egypt they say if you drink water from the Nile, you'll return. Here it's Saban rum. There's something magical about Saba."

Katche and Sable waited for Arthur to say more.

"People on this island stay in tune with the elements around them, and consequently live longer and happier lives," Arthur Teach went on. "I came here to die, you know. So far I haven't gotten around to it."

"You no die soon," Sable assured him.

"Quite," Arthur agreed. "The Teach family is long-lived, and so are my mother's people. I'm related to the pirate, you know," he confessed to Ruthana. "Blackbeard. We're quite proud to have him *hanging* on our family tree." Arthur chuckled at his own joke, pushing his empty cup toward Katche for a refill. "Do not spare the rum, girl."

"No, sir."

"How did your friend fare last night?" Arthur asked Ruthana.

"Quite well," Ruthana told him. "She got herself engaged to Sam."

Katche and Sable were round-eyed.

"Good for her," Arthur said. He gave Ruthana a shrewd glance. "That sort of romantic activity can be catching."

Ruthana laughed. "I believe I'm vaccinated."

Arthur smiled. "Don't be too sure of that, Miss Franklin."

Hugh had come down. "Did you get the note I left last night?" he asked Sable.

The big woman grinned and nodded.

"You and I are going on a New Year's Day picnic," Hugh announced to Ruthana.

"Are we?" she asked, surprised. "Where?"

"Somewhere," Hugh said. "We haven't decided yet."

Somewhere was Fort Bay with its beach and rolling surf. Seagulls wheeled and dived over the blue water just behind the breakers, adding their raucous calls to the roar of the surf, racing up the sand, and churning among the rocks.

Ruthana and Hugh had donned swimwear under their clothes. Ruthana's selection was the yellow bikini in which Hugh had first photographed her. He'd returned his costume wet suit and wore brief red trunks. When they'd selected a sheltered cove near Fort Bay and spread their picnic cloth at the mouth of a shallow cave, they stripped off their clothes to swim.

The water was surprisingly warm, and the sun was hot. Ruthana was always a strong swimmer, so she battled her way through the breaking waves to strike out. Hugh handled his long body well in the water and followed Ruthana's lead.

"Hey, you're good," was Hugh's comment about her swimming skill. "A regular waterbaby." They were treading water, side by side, looking in across the surf to the beach. "Where did you learn?"

"At school. I'm a pretty fair diver, too," Ruthana bragged. "Hugh?"

"What, Ruthana?"

"Did you take Whoever on a picnic the last time you were on Saba?"

"Hell, no!" Hugh laughed. "I've made some

mistakes about women in my time, but that little interlude was a real blooper."

Ruthana felt a twinge of jealousy. "Race you to the beach," she said.

"You're on."

Ruthana was ahead until a seventh wave caught her up in a smother of foam, rolled her along the sandy bottom, and left her gasping in its wake.

"Hey, are you all right?" Hugh had raced to her rescue. He stood over Ruthana in the shallow water. "You really caught it that time!"

"And you are telling *me*?" She sat on the bottom, arms crossed to cover her bare breasts. "Madame Yvonne's precious bra went that way. What do I do now?"

"Still got your pants?" Hugh asked.

"I think so." Ruthana looked down. "Yep. I'm decent below the waist. Fetch me a shirt?"

"No way." Hugh was grinning. "That, my girl, would spoil Venus rising from the waves, and I'm an art aficionado." Turning his back, Hugh waded to the beach, then turned and crossed his arms across his chest. "Coming?" he called. "You'll be pickled in brine if you sit out there the rest of the day like that."

"Laidman, you're a beast!" Ruthana squealed.

"A voyeur and Peeping Tom, too," Hugh called back. "Rise from the waves, girl, or are you waiting for me to get my camera?"

"Damn you, Laidman!" But there was nothing for it. "I hope you're struck blind!"

Ruthana stood up and, arms at her sides, waded to the beach. Hugh's appreciative stare somehow wasn't an embarrassment. Ruthana had secret pride about her body.

Hugh was the first man to see her bare to the waist.

"Hold it there," Hugh said in a subdued voice, when she was standing in front of him. "I'll be right back."

Ruthana covered her breasts with her arms and waited. *If he's gone for his camera, I'll kill him!* Ruthana thought.

Hugh brought back his shirt.

"Thanks, Hugh." She slipped into it. "You are a gentleman, after all. I was about to sell you short."

Hugh laughed, but then said in a sober voice, "You are, my darling, the most beautiful woman I've ever seen, and in my time I've seen a few."

"Are you bragging or confessing?" Ruthana asked.

"Neither," Hugh said. "I'm only stating a fact. Do you mind the comment?"

"I don't think so," Ruthana said.

They'd finished the picnic lunch Sable had packed and lay on their backs in the sun, side by side, forearms shielding their eyes. Hugh's shirt was dry now, and no longer revealing.

"Hugh?"

"Yes?"

"I thought you were asleep."

"I am," Hugh said. "What else do you want to know?"

"What was her name?" Ruthana asked.

"Whose name?"

"Miss Whoever. The one you brought the first time you came to Saba."

"Jealous?"

"A wee mite," Ruthana confessed.

"I've forgotten her name," Hugh said.

"Don't add lies to your other sins, Hugh."

"Okay. Her name was Gwendolyn. No last name available to you, dear. You might meet her one day. She's a model, but uses another first name."

Sandra Thompson! *Gwendolyn* had given Hugh's secret away. Ruthana had worked with her twice in the past month, a long-limbed, titian-haired, beautiful girl from Utica, New York.

"Imagine my dear mother and father tagging me with a first name like that!" Sandra Thompson had told Ruthana. "Are you sure your mother and father gave you Ruthana?"

"It's on my birth certificate," she'd told Sandra.

Ruthana had a perverse thought and had to stifle the giggle that might have given her away. It would certainly be amusing the next time she went on an assignment with Sandra!

Now that she knew the girl Hugh had brought to Saba, Ruthana's jealous twinge was gone. Somehow it endeared Hugh to her that he could be so frank about a mistake.

Hugh raised on an elbow to lean over and kiss Ruthana's lips. She returned his kiss without moving the forearm that shielded her eyes.

"Have I remembered to ask you to marry me

and have my children?" Hugh asked in a husky voice.

"I don't think so." She moved her arm so her eyes could meet his. "No. I remember now. You've only said that you love me."

"I'm a bit rueful about the way that came out," Hugh admitted.

"Ashamed?" she asked.

"Never! Rueful is something else."

"I know."

Golden flecks were deep in his eyes. She reached up and traced the firm line of his jaw with a finger. "This is my second marriage proposal."

"Philipe?" Hugh asked.

"No." Ruthana moved apart, to raise on her elbow, facing him. "A very stupid polo player and jet-set playboy wanted to march me down the middle aisle in a church of my choice."

"He sounds like a nice guy," Hugh said. "What did you tell him?"

Ruthana laughed. "I told Alex to shove it. He'd given me a bad time the night before," she said. "Came on very hot and heavy, but I wasn't having any, and I got my best dress ripped in the hassle. I had to use my knee, finally. That sort of thing doesn't really endear a man to a girl."

"I'll remember," Hugh promised. "What about Philipe Simon, Ruthana? Did you know that his sister hates you?"

"I've been getting those vibrations," Ruthana said. "She frightens me a little. Why do you suppose she dislikes me? I've never done anything to her."

"We could ask her," Hugh said.

"I don't think that's such a good idea, Hugh."

"I don't, either. Sibling rivalry?"

"Maybe, but I think it's more than that," Ruthana said. "She's talented as a painter. How she does as a witch I've no idea. Sam thinks she's pretty good in that department."

"Sam is a superstitious fool."

"Don't let Penny Andrews hear you say that about her man," Ruthana cautioned, "and don't try to point out that Sam is old enough to be her father."

"My kid sister married an older man and it turned out very well," Hugh said. "They have a farm that's a beauty, and the beginning of a family."

"Do you have many sisters?" Ruthana asked.

"No. Just Mary. No brothers, either. How about you?" he asked.

"I'm Mother's only child."

"I don't blame her for calling an early halt," Hugh said.

"Am I that bratty?"

"No." Hugh laughed. "Beautiful is the word. Your mother and father had created a masterpiece, so why try to top it?"

"Know something, Laidman?" Ruthana wrinkled her nose at him. "You've kissed whatever represents the Blarney stone where you come from. Flatter me some more?"

"Nope. Now it's your turn," Hugh said.

"You're a handsome man."

"Thank you. Go on."

"You take beautiful pictures," Ruthana said.

"That, too," Hugh told her. "But so do a few thousand other photographers. You can do better."

"You don't drink too much, and you can make a mean casserole. You don't try to push over every model who works for you. That's a big plus. Modeling can be a hazardous profession, you know. There are more wolves than sheep dogs out there."

162

"I'm a sheep dog?" Hugh asked with mock consternation. "I'll have to change that image!"

"You're not a dog." Ruthana patted his cheek. "You're a lamb. You also need a shave."

"No time this morning," Hugh said. "I had to get you away from The Castle before the Simons came down for breakfast. I heard Philipe tell Celeste last night they should have you for their houseguest a few days. So I kidnapped you."

"You're a true friend! Why not let me sort through my invitations, Laidman? I'm a big girl now. You should be ashamed of yourself!"

"Are you really angry?" Hugh asked, concerned.

"Not really," Ruthana admitted. "I don't think I want to know Celeste all that well."

"This conversation started with a simple proposal of marriage," Hugh said. "Let's go back and start over. You're supposed to come up with an answer to two important questions."

"Oh? And what might they be?"

"I love you," Hugh said. "Do you love me? That's question number one. Second question, I've asked you to marry me. Will you do it?"

Ruthana sat up and clasped her hands around

163

her knees. She stared out over the blue water. "I have to be very sure what my answer is to number one, Hugh, before I can possibly answer question number two."

"I understand that." Hugh stared at her profile. "You can't answer number one yet?"

"Not yet."

"Damn!" Hugh sat up and smacked a fist into his palm. "Let's get to the nitty-gritty. Do you love Simon? Okay, strike that one, it's none of my business where you and I stand right now. Let me ask it another way. Do you *want* the guy?"

Hugh was now on his feet, so Ruthana stood up, too. "You expect me to answer that, Laidman?" she asked in an angry voice.

"I've got a first name," Hugh snapped. "Try using it."

"Hugh," she said.

"Hugh, what?" His anger matched hers.

"You shouldn't have asked me that."

"Meaning you *do* want the guy? You've admitted that you're a big girl, Ruthana. The guy is attractive enough, and I'll admit it. If I were a girl . . ." Hugh stopped. "This is getting ridiculous!"

Ruthana's was a tentative smile. "We agree about that at any rate. Don't you suppose we should start back to The Castle?"

Hugh grinned. "Good idea, but I'm going in for a last plunge."

"Help yourself," Ruthana said, "but I'll pass this time."

"My shirt won't mind the wetting."

"I would," Ruthana said. "Your shirt is very transparent when wet, and you've seen enough of me for one day."

"Modesty, thy name is Ruthana!" Hugh exclaimed.

When they arrived back at The Castle in time for supper, Celeste and Philipe had left for Bottom. Penny obviously had something on her mind that was worrying her. "Can I see you in our room after supper?" she asked Ruthana.

"Yes, but what is it, Penny?"

"I'll tell you later."

When supper was over, Ruthana followed Penny upstairs. In the room Penny closed and locked the door.

"What is it, Penny?" Ruthana asked.

"Maybe nothing," Penny said. She pointed to

the dresser. "How many bras did you have in that top drawer?"

"Six. Why?"

"You'd better count them."

When Ruthana had finished, she discovered one was missing. "Did you borrow it?" Ruthana asked Penny.

"No," Penny said, "but I'm pretty sure that Celeste Simon did."

CHAPTER 11

Ruthana said, "That's ridiculous, Penny! Why would Celeste borrow one of my bras?"

"That I don't know. What I do know is that I came up here after breakfast because Sam wanted to call my folks in Pittsburgh, and I'd forgotten their number," Penny told Ruthana. "It was in my purse. I caught a glimpse of Celeste coming out of our room. She had something in her hand, and it looked like a bra."

"Did she see you?" Ruthana asked.

"I don't think she did. Anyway that drawer

wasn't closed tightly. One thing you're not is sloppy. I knew you had six bras, because I watched you unpack. So I looked in the drawer and counted only five."

Ruthana sank down to sit on the edge of her bed. "Have you told anyone else about this?" she asked.

Penny shook her head. "No. Not even Sam. I thought I could be mistaken, and Celeste got into the wrong room. How should I know Philipe's sister is a sneak thief?"

Remembering the bra incident in the surf that afternoon, Ruthana felt a shudder of cold fear, a completely irrational emotion, she told herself, but it was there.

"Do you suppose Celeste has a thing about other women's bras?" Penny asked. "Some men have what they call a fetish. I read about it in a book on abnormal psychology. Or maybe she's a klepto. One of the girls at the agency was arrested for shoplifting."

Ruthana studied Penny. She decided not to tell her about losing the yellow bikini bra. "I don't know what to think," she said. "I'm getting some pretty bad vibrations, Penny."

"So am I," Penny admitted. "You know that

for some reason Celeste doesn't like you, don't you?"

"I have that impression," Ruthana said.

"What if she really is a witch, Ruthana?"

"I don't know."

"My Sam is a pretty reasonable man," Penny said. "He's certain Celeste is a witch."

"That's crazy, Penny. We don't believe in witchcraft since Salem and those poor women." Ruthana was trying to convince herself as much as she was Penny. "She could have all my bras, if she asked."

"She doesn't wear your size cup, Ruthana."

"There is that," Ruthana admitted.

"This model I told you about was caught stealing safety pins! Can you imagine? She didn't even have a baby to diaper. The last I heard she was still going to a shrink. Maybe Celeste *is* a kleptomaniac. Can you ask Philipe?" Penny said. "Hey! Speaking of Philipe, when you two left together the other night, Laidman was chewing the carpet in his quiet, jealous way."

"You haven't told him anything, have you?" Ruthana asked.

"Of course not," Penny said. "But I have been

thinking about what you told me—it being impossible to marry."

Ruthana nodded. "He told me marriage is out for some reason having to do with his sister."

"I'll bet she isn't his sister," Penny said. "For twins they sure don't look alike."

"You've just opened a whole new vista," Ruthana told Penny. "Philipe could be married to the woman."

"My Sam would know if he was. He knows about everything here on Saba. Why don't we ask him?"

"You could," Ruthana said. "I wouldn't know how to bring it up."

Penny frowned. "I can see your point. But Sam is worried about you."

"He's told you that?"

Penny nodded. "Last night in bed." Penny's hand jumped to her mouth, and she turned scarlet. "I didn't *say* that!"

"Then I didn't hear it," Ruthana said.

Penny perched on the edge of her bed. "Ruthana, we're going to be married in a week. That's why Sam talked with Daddy. My Sam is old-fashioned in some ways. It was all my fault last night happened. He says I can still wear white to our wedding."

"Penny, I'm delighted that you and Sam found a unique way to celebrate New Year's Eve," Ruthana said. She wanted to ask a question, but thought better of it. "The next time you and Sam go to bed, ask him about Celeste, will you? It's sort of a pillow-talk thing."

"Oh, wow!" Penny's eyes sparkled. "If I need an excuse for an encore, you've given me one." She hesitated, then said in a whisper, "The first time hurts like hell, Ruthana, so the right man is very important."

Penny had answered the question Ruthana didn't ask. "I thank you for that information," she said.

"Are you going to be Philipe's mistress?" Penny asked.

Ruthana was shocked to discover she couldn't give a Yes or No answer to that question. *My whole moral code is breaking down,* she thought. *Hugh wants marriage, so what is there to decide?*

Hugh also wanted children.

"I shouldn't have asked that," Penny said. "Strike the question. What did he and Hugh do to you at the party, or should I strike that question, too?"

"No. Let it stand. They didn't do anything to me. I just got emotional. Maybe it was the drinks, I just don't know."

"You don't drink that much," Penny said. "You don't know which man you love, do you?"

Ruthana nodded. "Isn't that crazy? I've been so sure I'd recognize Mister Right when he came along. Now I'm not sure of anything, least of all myself."

"You'll know when the right time comes," Penny assured her.

"I wish I could be sure of that, but right now I feel fickle and foolish," Ruthana said. "I just *can't* be in love with two different men at the same time! Can I?"

"If you're not, you could have fooled me," Penny said with a laugh. Then she dropped a stone in the quiet pool of Ruthana's mind. "So Celeste has your bra. Do you suppose she's at home sticking pins in it right now?"

"Cut that out, Penny!"

"Come to think of it, why would she need your bra?" Penny asked. "She has that portrait of you, and it *is* you, Ruthana. I think that Katerina ghost story is a lot of flack."

"You've just made my day," Ruthana said.

Sam knocked. "Are you all right, Penny?"

"Just a minute," Penny sang out and went to unlock the door. "I'm just fine, honey," she said. "Come on in. We were just having a girl-talk session. Nothing important."

"Philipe phoned a few minutes ago," Sam told Ruthana. "He was in a hurry so he gave me the message. Something important has come up. He wants to see you this evening and will drop by at seven."

Ruthana thanked Sam for the message.

"Should I ask him now?" Penny said.

"Go ahead," Ruthana told her.

"Sam, it's about Celeste and Philipe Simon. Are they really twins? Or is it possible they are secretly married or maybe living together?"

Sam hesitated, tugging at the lobe of his ear. "Do you know I've never given much thought to what you're suggesting, but if they aren't siblings that would explain a lot of things."

"How can we find out?" Penny asked.

"Birth records?" Ruthana suggested.

"Doubtful," Sam said. "Philipe handled that

chore for De Graaf and the administrator before him. The pair of them owned a choice piece of oceanfront over on Saint Martin but sold it for a condominium that's being built by a Dutch outfit. Herr Brinker was the lawyer who handled the details, and I know him pretty well. I'll make some inquiries."

"Please do that," Ruthana said.

"Philipe's status is important to you, isn't it?" Sam said. "He's done me a few favors, and I haven't a thing against the man, but go slowly in his direction, Ruthana. He's used to getting everything he wants, and it's pretty obvious that Philipe wants you."

"I must wear my heart on my sleeve!" Ruthana said.

"No." Sam grinned. "It's just that running a place like The Castle gives you insights. To an innkeeper, guests are much more transparent than they think. We're a special breed."

With Sam and Penny gone, Ruthana soaked in a hot tub, then slipped into her favorite pantsuit and brushed her freshly shampooed hair. Her color was so good after a day in the sun that Ruthana didn't use any makeup.

Downstairs she found Hugh changed and waiting for her. "What say we drive up to the airport?" he said. "I've heard you get a magnificent view of Saba from there, before the generator shuts down."

"Hugh, thanks, but I can't," Ruthana said.

"Simon?"

"Yes."

Hugh grinned sheepishly. "Odd man out."

"I'm not playing a game, Hugh," Ruthana said. "He has something important he wants to talk about."

"Let me guess."

"I wish you wouldn't," she told him.

"I won't, then," Hugh promised. "I'll just sit in the patio and drown my jealousy in good Saban rum. Who knows? I might just succeed."

"Then again," Ruthana said, smiling, "you might just succeed in getting yourself drunk."

"Laidman drunk isn't an edifying spectacle," Hugh said. "If I stayed sober at the bash last night, I guess I can manage tonight, but don't count on it."

"Count on what, Laidman?" Philipe had come in. Ruthana thought that he was pale and that there was something rigid about the expression

175

on his face. He might just as well have been wearing a mask. "I'm half an hour late," Philipe told Ruthana. "Sorry about that but it couldn't be helped. Car trouble."

"I needed the extra time to get decent," Ruthana told him.

"I'll be seeing you." Hugh drifted toward the patio.

In the car Philipe drove toward Hell's Gate. Whatever he wanted to discuss, the Volkswagen wasn't the place for it. The top was down, and the night air smelled of flowers. From the side of the road Clarence stared at them balefully as they passed. This time Philipe didn't park in front of his brick home. Instead he drove around in back, to park in shrubbery so the car would be unnoticed from the main road.

"You're being mysterious tonight," Ruthana said.

"No. Just bloody careful," Philipe said. He reached for a rolled canvas on the backseat that Ruthana hadn't noticed. "Let's go in the house."

There was no fire this time and no good smell of food. All windows were closed, as well as the steel hurricane shutters. The cold air trapped inside the house smelled stale.

On the table in front of the fireplace, where they'd shared supper, Philipe unrolled the canvas and weighted it with ashtrays.

"Come closer," he urged Ruthana. "I want you to see this."

An involuntary shudder wracked Ruthana, and there was suddenly a cold ball of fear in the pit of her stomach. The flickering candles Philipe had lighted cast weird shadows on the room's walls. On leaden feet she moved to the table, standing beside Philipe, to stare down at the painting.

The arms and body in the black dress were the same, so Ruthana recognized the painting —but the head and face!

The glow of beauty had been painted out. In its place there was a greenish-white face of a dead woman, rotting teeth clenched in a rictus of final agony, once blonde hair now white.

"My God!" Ruthana was looking at her own dead face. The cold ball of fear exploded, and Ruthana was drenched with perspiration, yet shivering as if she had a chill.

"Are you all right?" Philipe's protective arm was around her waist.

"I don't know." Ruthana's hands, palms down

on the tabletop, compensated for her watery knees. "I'm seeing myself dead, and I can't stop looking."

Philipe lifted the ashtrays. The painting rolled itself up. This time he gathered shuddering Ruthana to him. "You'll see, it's going to be all right." He comforted her. "Celeste has something very personal that belongs to you, Ruthana. Do you know what it is?"

"Yes." She spoke against his chest. Her voice was muffled. "It's one of my bras."

"What?"

Ruthana looked up into Philipe's face. "She took . . . stole . . . one of my brassieres, Philipe. I'd only worn it once. Penny saw her coming from our room."

His jaw tightened. "Damn!" Philipe spoke through clenched teeth. "I was afraid this would happen. I never should have brought her to The Castle. You see, Celeste knows how much I love you. She was here the other night."

"Here? You mean when we had supper?" Ruthana asked.

"Yes."

"But that's impossible! Another person in this

small house and we wouldn't know it? I can't believe that."

Philipe's arms were still around Ruthana. "There's a scientific word for it," he said. "Teleportation. Celeste has the Power. She's told me everything we said and did, even what you wore. I didn't find out until today. We had quite a grim scene."

"Philipe, tell me something." Ruthana moved out of his arms. "Exactly what is your relationship with Celeste? Can you be completely honest? I might be able to love you, if you were. As it is, I'm just plain afraid to let myself go."

"Sit down over there." Philipe nodded to a leather couch at the opposite end of the small living room. "Excuse me a minute. Do you want a drink?"

"No."

"I need one." Philipe disappeared into the kitchen. In a moment he was back, with a double shot of rum in his hand. He silently paced the length of the room while Ruthana waited.

Standing with an elbow on the mantel of the fireplace, Philipe tossed down the rum and set aside the glass.

"I don't know how to begin. You see I've never told this to anyone, Ruthana." Philipe placed a fist over his heart. "It hurts in here."

"Is Celeste your sister?" Ruthana asked.

"No."

"Ruthana's heart lurched and sank.

"She's my first cousin," Philipe said. "We were born the same night, at exactly the same time, and both our mothers died in childbirth. They died only minutes apart."

"Was this here on Saba?" Ruthana asked.

"No. Our families lived on Saint Vincent then. Do you know anything about the *Morro Castle* disaster?" Philipe asked. "It was before your time."

"I don't," Ruthana admitted. "Was it a hotel fire?"

"No. It was a cruise ship. It caught on fire and burned off the New Jersey coast. My father was a purser on the *Morro Castle*. He burned to death, or was drowned; we never found out which. Celeste's father took me in and brought us to Saba."

"Is he alive?" Ruthana asked.

"No. He drowned at Fort Bay, trying to bring cargo ashore. We were sixteen. I'd promised

Celeste's father I would take care of her for the rest of our lives," Philipe said. "He made me swear that on a Bible and crucifix the night before he drowned. You see he knew. You can believe that or not. Take your choice. But it's true."

"I believe it," Ruthana said, hands in her lap, knees together. "But why can't Celeste make her own way in the world, Philipe?"

Philipe lit a cigarette. There was wood in the fireplace, and he stooped to light it. "Can you bring me another double?" he asked.

"Surely."

In the kitchen Ruthana poured the drink, then brought it back to Philipe.

"Thank you, darling," he said. "Cheers."

They turned their backs to the fire. Philipe had pushed aside the table with the rolled canvas on it. Ruthana nodded toward the macabre painting. "Can't we burn it?" she asked.

"Sure." Philipe poked the rolled-up canvas into the fire.

It didn't catch immediately.

When it did, acrid smoke swirled out of the fireplace with a stench of burning paint and cloth. It followed them as they retreated to the other end of the room. Philipe threw open a window. Cool night air poured in.

"What's wrong with Celeste?" Ruthana asked.

Philipe was a long time answering. "She is, for one thing, an insanely jealous woman," he said, when he finally began. "I brought a woman here, to this house, four years ago. I'm not proud of that, Ruthana."

"You shouldn't be."

"You may have noticed her grave in the front yard, near the palmetto."

CHAPTER 12

Ruthana's heart beat faster, and blood sang in her ears, but she kept her voice level. "I didn't notice a grave, Philipe. Who was she, and how did she die?"

"The girl's name was Felice. I met her on Saint Vincent and brought her to Saba. Felice was just seventeen, but she had no family. She was nearly as beautiful as you, but I didn't love her and told Felice that, but she came to Saba with me anyway."

Philipe lit another cigarette. Ruthana noticed

that his hands trembled. "Three weeks later Felice was dead."

"How did she die?" Ruthana asked again.

"Celeste *willed* her to die. Can you believe that?" Philipe asked. "It was a massive cerebral hemorrhage, the doctor said, but I know better."

"I just can't believe your cousin has that much power over life and death," Ruthana said. "I'm sorry, Philipe."

He threw his cigarette in the fire. "You had better believe it," he said. "Celeste is somewhere on Saba, willing your death right now."

"You don't know where she is?" Ruthana asked.

"No. We had a terrible scene when I found what she'd done to your portrait, and she stormed out of the house. There are at least a dozen families on the island who would hide her from me. They would be afraid of what she might do if they didn't."

Unreasonable fear gnawed Ruthana. The girl's death, she assured herself, was from natural causes, but a stroke at seventeen? *Now I'm being childish*, she thought. *I'll have to believe she's a witch for Celeste to harm me.*

Philipe's hands caught her shoulders, and

their eyes met. "Leave Saba with me on the morning plane, Ruthana." His voice was husky with emotion. "We can be married and never come back."

For a long moment Ruthana found herself willing to surrender her life and body to Philipe, but the moment passed, and she looked away. "You're Saba's administrator," she reminded Philipe. "The island is your home. We can't run away, don't you see that?"

"You don't know how much danger there is for you here," Philipe said. "I have money. I could take you back to New York, if that's your wish. Celeste won't follow us because she can't leave Saba."

"Why can't she leave Saba if you can?" Ruthana asked. "That doesn't make sense, Philipe."

"Celeste is too afraid of the outside world. She went to Saint Martin with me once, to sign some important papers, and nearly died of fright," Philipe told Ruthana. "Her fear is a very real thing."

"Agoraphobia, isn't it?" Ruthana answered. "I've heard of people like that. She can be cured."

Philipe gathered Ruthana to him and kissed

her passionately. The wish to surrender came
back stronger than before as she began returning his kisses. Ruthana broke away from his
encircling arms, brushing hair away from her
face.

"Will you marry me tomorrow?" Philipe
asked. "We can be married on Saint Martin
and honeymoon on Bermuda."

"Celeste would always be between us,
Philipe," Ruthana said. "You should know that
better than I. Anyway, I'm a working girl on
an assignment, and I couldn't let Hugh Laidman down." She continued marshaling reasons
why she couldn't marry Philipe. "There's my
mother in Philadelphia. She will have to know
before I marry. That much I owe her. And I
don't want a runaway marriage, because it's
going to be a lifetime commitment for me."

"You just don't love me enough." Philipe was
bitter. "If you did, none of these other things
would matter. Be honest with me, Ruthana. You
don't love me, do you?"

She turned away, to hide her face from him.
His intent stare had begun to hypnotize her.
"My honest answer, Philipe, is that I just don't
know, and until I do, I won't promise you, or

anyone else, anything. We'd better take me back to The Castle."

"You won't be safe there," Philipe said.

"I'm not safe here," Ruthana told him, with a shy smile. "I'll have to take my chances with Celeste at The Castle." For the first time in her life Ruthana had a precognitive thought. "She'll come there tomorrow."

Philipe was in one of his silent moods during the short drive from Hell's Gate to The Castle, and Ruthana stayed lost in her own thoughts.

"Will I see you tomorrow?" Philipe asked when he let her out of the car.

"I'll be working all day."

"I have my work," Philipe said. "Tomorrow night?"

"I don't know, Philipe. I may be very tired. Why don't you call me?"

Philipe promised that he would.

Hugh was on the patio, nursing a nightcap. He invited Ruthana to join him. "No questions will be asked," Hugh promised. "I'm on my gentlemanly behavior tonight. What will you have? Manuel's gone to bed, but Sam has turned the bar over to me."

"Just a little wine, Hugh."

The generator was turned off, so the patio was lit with hurricane lanterns. The battery-operated radio was tuned to a Jamaican station and turned low.

"There's a tropical storm brewing somewhere out there," Hugh reported when he'd brought her wine and another nightcap for himself. "Sam says our barometer is headed for the cellar. We may have a hurricane to entertain us within the next forty-eight hours. I've never experienced one of those."

"Neither have I," Ruthana said. "I don't know about a hurricane being entertainment. Do we work tomorrow?"

"Like beavers," Hugh laughed. "Just in case the weather turns bad on us. I've sent what we've shot already off to New York for processing. I may have to go up there for a day."

"Why?" Ruthana asked.

"For a conference with Madame Yvonne. She called earlier this evening. She's adding a line of children's wear for this spring and wants me to include some of those styles. Sam has promised to dig me up some local kids to pose.

That shouldn't be too hard. I've seen quite a few nice-looking kids since we arrived."

"I have, too," Ruthana said. She sipped her wine. "This is good. What's the label?"

"I don't know. It's dark in there behind the bar. I tasted two wines, and this was the best."

"What time did Penny go up to bed?" Ruthana asked.

"About half an hour ago," Hugh said. "She wanted to see you about something, but got too sleepy."

Ruthana finished her wine. "I better join her."

"Do I get a good-night kiss for sitting up and staying sober?" Hugh asked.

"You do." Ruthana took his face between her palms and kissed him firmly. "Will that do?"

Hugh considered before answering. "No." He drew her down on his lap. His lips touched the soft hollow of her throat, then her chin; finally they found her lips.

Ruthana's arms crept around his neck. One of the hurricane lamps sputtered. It was Hugh who finally lifted her from his lap to her feet. "Go along upstairs before I forget I'm a gentleman tonight," he said. "Sweet dreams."

* * *

Penny was awake. Ruthana undressed by candlelight. "How did it go with Philipe tonight?" Penny asked.

"He wanted to tell me that Celeste is trying to cast a death spell," Ruthana said. "She's hiding somewhere on Saba. They had a quarrel." Ruthana told Penny about the death portrait and that Philipe had burned it. "He also asked me to leave Saba with him and get married."

"Wow!"

"I put him off," Ruthana confessed. "Penny, I'm in more of a spin than ever. How do I straighten up and fly right? I'm being a little fool!"

"You could flip a coin," Penny said.

"Big help you are!" Ruthana threatened her with a pillow.

Penny cowered. "Only kidding." Penny sat up and was serious. "This Celeste thing has me worried, Ruthana. How do you feel?"

"Tired."

"You don't hurt anywhere?"

"No. Stop believing she can do anything to me. I think that this witchcraft thing is a lot of nonsense and that Philipe's a little crazy to believe it."

"He knows his sister better than you do."

"Celeste is a first cousin, not his sister," Ruthana told her. "Just before they became orphans, Philipe promised her father he'd take care of Celeste. He says she's insanely jealous."

"I wonder why." Penny said.

"That's one little thing that has me wondering, too," Ruthana said. "I need to talk with Celeste. She'll be here sometime tomorrow."

"You've heard from her?" Penny asked.

"No. I just know she'll come here to The Castle," Ruthana said. Ruthana blew out the candle and slipped into her bed. "Good night, Penny."

"Good night. Laidman will be pounding on our door early," she said. "He has big ideas for us all day tomorrow."

"He told me."

"Did you tell him Philipe proposed?" Penny asked.

"No. That wouldn't be fair to Philipe or Hugh. Not the way I see it. Good night again, Penny."

191

* * *

It was dark and cold. Ruthana sat up to reach the extra blanket at the foot of her bed, then froze. She'd locked the room door herself, shooting the bolt, but now it was open. That was causing the cold draft. *Something or someone is waiting out there in the corridor for me*, she thought.

She had a spasm of cold fear.

Penny was fast asleep, breathing evenly in the dark, cold room.

Should she explore the corridor? Maybe wind had blown the door open. The trouble with that theory was there was no wind, not even a breeze. It was like weather on Saba held its breath, waiting for hurricane winds.

Ruthana got up and, with her feet, found her slippers, then slipped on her robe.

From the doorway she peered up and down the corridor. A sputtering hurricane lantern was hanging at the head of the stairs. It shed just enough light for Ruthana to see the corridor was empty, but the feeling that she wasn't the only one awake persisted. Squaring her shoulders, Ruthana walked toward the stairs. Someone could be on them, out of sight.

No one was. Ruthana stood for a moment, a hand on the banister. She was suddenly aware that out here it was no longer cold. The night, as a matter of fact, was still and warm.

Suddenly the girl was off-balance, as if she'd been pushed, and only Ruthana's grip on the banister saved her from a nasty fall downstairs. She staggered back from the head of the stairs, to spin around.

There was only the empty corridor.

I'm flipping!, Ruthana thought. But she remembered Sam's story about the guest who thought he'd been pushed out a window.

A gust of wind that seemed to come from nowhere slammed the open room door and startled Ruthana so that she bumped the wall with her shoulder. Rubbing that shoulder, she walked to her room and tried the door. It was bolted from inside!

"Penny," Ruthana whispered, then raised her voice. "Penny, let me in."

There was no response. Ruthana tapped lightly on the door. "Penny?"

The hurricane lantern at the head of the stairs sputtered, popped, and went out to leave Ruthana in darkness. Fear, worse than anything she'd felt before, caused Ruthana to call out "Penny Adrews!" She slapped the door hard, with the heel of her hand. "Let me in!"

The movement was directly behind her! Ruthana spun around, shoulders against the door, a scream ready to burst from her throat.

"What's going on?" Sam Lord asked. He snapped on his flashlight. "I heard someone prowling around up here. Was that you?"

Penny picked that moment to throw open the door, and Ruthana fell back into her arms.

"It was me." Ruthana sighed with relief; she waited for her heart to stop pounding. "I nearly fell down the stairs."

Sam moved past the girls into their room to light a lantern. Penny found her robe and slippers. All the coldness she'd originally felt had gone from their room, Ruthana noticed.

She settled in a chair, taking a deep breath.

Sam was fully dressed in khaki pants and a shirt open at the throat, but he was barefoot. Ruthana realized that was why she didn't hear him come upstairs. Tucked in the belt of his trousers was a wicked-looking automatic.

"Is it loaded?" Ruthana pointed to the

weapon, then realized she'd asked an inane question. "Sorry. I'm still upset."

"I don't hunt prowlers with an unloaded gun," Sam said, "but settle down. I haven't shot a guest of mine yet." He was standing just inside the doorway. "Do you want to tell us about it, Ruthana? You've had quite a scare."

Ruthana pressed her hands to her cheeks for a moment. "I woke up and it was cold in here," she said. "When I reached for my extra blanket, I noticed the door was wide open."

"Cold?" Sam frowned. "This is one of the warmest nights we've had."

"I felt it was cold," Ruthana said. "I got up to close the door, then thought someone might be in the corridor, so I looked. I walked to the head of the stairs and nearly fell down them. Then that room door slammed. Somehow it was bolted. And that's all of it."

"Honey, the door wasn't bolted," Penny said.

"I couldn't open it."

Sam tried the door. It opened and closed easily. He examined the bolt, working it a few times. "Nothing wrong here," he said. "Ruthana, I don't want you to go anywhere alone, do you understand? Nowhere. Have someone with you at all times. I know about Celeste and what she's trying to do. We'll find some way to stop her, but in the meantime, be very careful."

"I don't believe this is happening to me!" Ruthana said. "There has to be a reasonable explanation. Philipe is afraid for me, too."

"He should be," Sam said in a dry voice. "His attention to you has set her off this time."

"Did you know she's his cousin and not a sister?" Penny asked Sam.

"No. How did you find that out?" Sam asked.

"He told me tonight," Ruthana said.

Arthur Teach, in robe and slippers, his hair tousled, looked in on them. "I heard a bit of commotion," he said. "What seems to be our problem?"

"Ruthana is being hexed," Sam explained.

"Is that so?" Arthur's eyebrows went up. "We do have a problem then. It's Celeste Simon, I assume. She's an unfortunate woman." Arthur patted a yawn. "What do we intend to do about this?" he asked Sam.

"Look, all you people, I refuse to believe any part of this witchcraft business," Ruthana broke in. "It's absolutely silly to think Celeste Simon can will me into having some sort of accident or dropping dead. She'll come here tomorrow. I'll talk with her then and get this matter settled."

"How do you know she'll come here?" Sam asked.

"I just know it," Ruthana said. "Now let's all get some sleep."

She slept soundly and without dreaming for the rest of the night.

The next day the sky was cloudless and bluer than Ruthana had ever seen it before. They worked in the streets of Windwardside and out on the brink of the cliff, toward the end of the day. Hugh wanted the dark blue sky as a backdrop. Penny had a fear of heights. There was a narrow ledge a few feet from the brow of the cliff. By climbing down and standing on it, Hugh managed some original camera angles, but Ruthana had to do all the posing.

To stay in camera range she had to foot along the edge.

"Laidman, she's going to fall off, and you are, too," Penny called, a safe ten feet back from the edge. "Both of you are fruitcakes."

"Just a few more exposures," Hugh told

Ruthana. "Look up as if you're watching sea gulls. Turn just a hair to the right. There it is. Hold it." He snapped the Rolleiflex and rolled the film. "One more."

Breaking her pose, Ruthana stepped too close to the edge, and ground broke away under her feet. She heard Penny's scream, and Hugh's startled exclamation as she began to fall.

CHAPTER 13

Ruthana fell into Hugh's arms. The strap holding the camera snapped when she hit him, and it fell and smashed on the rocks below. They teetered on the ledge. Hugh grabbed at a bush, Ruthana got her feet down and found the ledge.

The bush tore out of the face of the cliff.

Both of them were falling. Ruthana twisted free of his grasp. With toes and fingers she tore at the face of the cliff. A rock, poking out from the cliff, broke her fall for a moment, but then it gave way, and Ruthana, on her back, was sliding down toward the rocks below.

Hugh managed two running steps, then arched out from the cliff.

Ruthana hit another ledge with her feet. Arms spread, body pressed against the rocky wall, she saw Hugh dive into a rising swell at the foot of the cliff. He surfaced. A kick and a few strokes and he was below her, looking up.

Clothes plastered to his body, Hugh was in knee-deep water, as the swell subsided. Then another rolled in. It lifted him; he grabbed at a slippery rock, somehow hung on.

"Ruthana." Over the sucking sound of the surging water she heard Hugh clearly. She was face-out on the ledge, and a good thirty feet separated her from the rocks and water. "Wait. Dive when I say."

She didn't dare nod, or even speak. Pebbles were pattering down the cliff's face all around her. Hugh measured a rising swell, yelled "Now!"

She couldn't. Terror froze her against the face of the cliff. She was wearing a brief bikini and felt as if her arms, legs, and body had been sandpapered.

"Okay, Ruthana." Crouched on the slimy rock, Hugh stared up. He was trying to soothe her. "You're going to be all right. Don't freeze up there. Next time dive when I say."

"Ruthana!" Penny wailed. Sprawled full-length on the ground above, Penny was peering over the edge.

"Stupid!" Hugh shouted up to Penny. "Get help."

"Right." Penny was gone.

"Please, Ruthana," Hugh pleaded. "You have to dive when I say, baby." Another swell was rising as it rolled toward the base of the cliff. "You can do it. *Now!*"

Before she knew what was happening, Ruthana was in the air, arms spread. She knifed into the crest of the swell, touched bottom, kicked her way to the surface. Hugh grabbed her. He pushed her up on a flattop boulder, then hoisted himself to gather her shivering body against his own.

"That was too close, baby." Hugh kissed her chin, her forehead, finally her salty lips.

Sam Lord was up above. "You, down there."

"What?" Hugh yelled back.

"We're getting a rope." Sam yelled through cupped hands. "Can she walk up?"

"I don't know."

"What's he talking about?" Ruthana asked. Her teeth chattered. "I'm cold!"

"Sam is going to drop down a bowline noose in the rope," Hugh explained. "We slip it over your head and under your arms. Then all you have to do is walk up the face of the cliff. No big deal."

"So you say! I can't do it," Ruthana told him.

"Don't go helpless on me, Ruthana. You can do it, and you'd better. I don't want to stay down here all night."

"Rope coming down," Sam called.

"Keep your legs stiff," Hugh cautioned when he'd adjusted the noose and retied the bowline knot. "Go, baby." Hugh lifted her, she found footing on the cliff, the rope tightened. "Bye, bye."

Hugh gave her bottom a friendly pat.

"Fresh!" Ruthana said down to him.

Hugh grinned and blew a kiss.

Penny folded Ruthana in a blanket when she came up over the cliff's edge. A group of a dozen men had gathered to help with the rope. Sam sent it back down for Hugh.

Ruthana gulped from the rum bottle thrust into her hands, choked, coughed, then felt the spreading warmth that radiated from her stomach. Her teeth stopped chattering so she could talk.

"Ruthana fall down." From childhood she'd dredged that phrase. Ruthana giggled. "How is Hugh making it?" she asked Penny.

"You think I'm going to look?" Penny said. "I'm not that crazy!"

Hugh came scrambling over the edge to solid ground. He grabbed Sam's hand. "That was quick thinking."

"I was at The Lido."

"Lucky for us." Hugh came to Ruthana. He tilted the rum bottle handed him. "As Penny would say, wow!" Hugh wiped his mouth with the back of his hand and returned the bottle to the elderly Saban. "I really needed that."

"What do you mean, calling me stupid?" Penny asked, and she was angry.

"Hey, Penny, I'm sorry."

"You ought to be." She smiled. "Laidman, I'm sorry about your camera."

"Think nothing of it." Hugh's eyes searched Ruthana's face. "You did pretty well down there, girl," he said. "That was a nice, clean dive. I'd give you nine points in competition."

"Why not ten?" Ruthana asked.

Hugh grinned and patted her cheek. "Nobody's perfect."

Sam joined the three of them. "Well, that's the matinee," he said. "What do you two have in mind for the evening show?"

"Don't sell any tickets," Hugh said. His arm was around Ruthana. "Let me walk you home, baby."

They were in the patio after supper. Sam had broken out a bottle of Chivas Regal Scotch for Hugh, Arthur, and himself. Penny and Ruthana were enjoying Manuel's rum punch.

"She'll come through at about midnight," Sam told them. He sniffed the air. "Smells like brass, doesn't it? Saint Vincent got a whipping, but Barbuda caught the full blast of Estelle. Winds up to two-hundred miles per hour, or so they claim."

"I'm scared," Penny said.

"Me, too," Ruthana confessed.

204

"Saba won't blow away," Sam assured them. "We've had plenty of warning. Everything on the island is tied down or buttoned up."

"Quite," Arthur agreed. "Sabans are used to these hurricanes. They're a hardy lot, these chaps. Sable and Katche are burning palm fronds all over The Castle."

"Why are they doing that?" Ruthana asked.

"I can't say with exactitude where that particular superstition originated," Arthur said, "but it may have something to do with Palm Sunday, which more or less marks the beginning of the hurricane season."

"I didn't know hurricanes had seasons," Penny said.

"Oh, yes," Arthur said. "Estelle is out of season, you know. From early summer until mid-fall is the usual hurricane season."

"Wow!" Penny said. "We would come down here just in time for a freaky storm."

"The first blow should last an hour at most," Sam said. "Then we're in the eye of the storm. The second blast will be as bad, or worse, than the first, but it won't last as long. We'll probably get rain like you've never seen."

"Hurricanes are simply cyclones with stronger

winds," Arthur told them. "They would look like a doughnut, seen from space. The calm eye is the hole in the doughnut. When it has passed, the thrust of the wind is in the opposite direction, usually."

"My wine cellar is blasted out of solid rock," Sam said. "If Estelle gets too bad, we can retreat there to wait her out."

"I don't think it's fair to name hurricanes after us women," Penny told them. "Some male chauvinist dreamed that up."

"Probably," Hugh said. "Yet they're fickle enough." He was looking at Ruthana. "And they do sweep men off their feet."

Ruthana sipped her rum punch, avoiding Hugh's stare. She was facing the patio entrance from the house. The backs of the others were to it, so Ruthana saw Celeste in the shadows first. The woman was swathed in an ankle-length black cape, with a hood over her head. With no word to the others, Ruthana rose and walked toward Celeste.

Celeste moved back into the hallway that reached from the front of The Castle to the patio. Ruthana followed her. "Hello, Celeste," she said. "I've been expecting you."

The woman's face was void of any expression. Only her eyes seemed alive. "You've forced me to come," Celeste said. "Why?"

"So we can talk." *If she wants to believe I've summoned her,* Ruthana thought, *so much the better.* "Let's go to my room upstairs. We won't be disturbed there."

Celeste meekly followed Ruthana. When the door was bolted, Celeste sat in a straight-backed chair. Ruthana sat on the edge of the bed, facing Celeste.

"Does your cousin know you're here?" Ruthana asked.

"No. We've had a very bad quarrel. Philipe banished me from our home." Celeste's eyes were luminous. "It was a very wicked thing for him to do."

Ruthana was startled to realize there were tears in Celeste's eyes. She found herself deeply touched. But she didn't know what she could say that would reach a responsive chord in the woman. She'd seen those tragic eyes, baleful and filled with hate, but never before with unshed tears.

Celeste sat primly straight, hands on her knees, and somehow reminded Ruthana of an

Egyptian goddess. She leaned toward Celeste and covered the woman's hands with her own.

"You're ice cold!" Ruthana exclaimed. "Where have you been all this time?"

"In a cave near here," Celeste said.

"All alone?"

Celeste nodded. "Philipe would have found me, otherwise. I can no longer trust anyone on Saba."

"You can trust me," Ruthana said.

"After what I've tried to do to you?" Celeste asked. "I've wanted you to die, like his other woman. I killed her, you know."

"A doctor said you didn't." Ruthana reasoned with Celeste. "I don't believe you did."

"You nearly fell downstairs last night and might have broken your neck. Then you fell from the cliff this afternoon."

"How do you know these things?" Ruthana asked.

Celeste's was a ghostly smile. "I have second sight. I always have."

"I believe you," Ruthana said, "but we both know you aren't into witchcraft, don't we?"

Celeste didn't answer. She'd blinked back the tears. Her color was better.

"Tell me about you and Philipe," Ruthana urged her. "You must love him very much."

"I always have."

This simple statement from Celeste's lips overwhelmed Ruthana with pity, and tears smarted in her eyes. "Is there any law down here that says first cousins can't marry?" she asked Celeste.

"No." A smile brightened her face. "On these small Caribbean islands everyone is related in some way to everyone else. Such a law would be impossible. But you may have noticed that my mother was not all white."

Ruthana had understood, before coming to Saba, that there was a general mixture of races in the West Indies, but on this island there were whites, and there were Negroes, but very few people of mixed color. The girl, Katche, was an exception. Sable was a typical black Saban.

Ruthana considered this in the light of what she had just heard. "Which one of your cousins objects to that?" she asked.

"I do." Celeste lifted her head proudly. "My cousin has noble blood in his veins. We are descended from French men and women shipwrecked on Saba while fleeing the French Revolution."

"You have the same noble blood," Ruthana reminded her. "Tell me about your mother."

"She was a very proud and handsome woman. I loved her very much. My father called her his black goddess. When she died. . . ." Celeste made a helpless gesture with her hands.

"So why are you ashamed of her blood?" Ruthana asked.

"I'm not!"

"Has Philipe asked you to marry him?" Ruthana said.

"Many times in the past."

"But not lately?"

"No. When we sold our property on Saint Martin he wanted me to stay there, or on some other island with him, as his wife, but I couldn't. I'm trapped here on Saba," Celeste said.

The storm of indecision that had been raging in Ruthana's breast was suddenly calmed. She finally knew with whom she was in love! She wanted to kiss Celeste and thank her, but Ruthana kept her cool poise. She searched for words, because what she was going to tell Celeste would change the other woman's life, and

Philipe's, too. *Could* change their lives, Ruthana amended.

"Celeste, I'm younger than you are," Ruthana began. "I don't have your great talent, and it is just that. You are blessed. Your painting of Katerina, or whoever, has been burned, and that's my fault. I don't know how to make it up to you. But you can paint another portrait, and another."

Celeste was listening intently. Ruthana had never had anyone hang on her words like this.

"Here's what I want you to do. I want you to accept a commission to paint me again, this time from life. The portrait will be for my mother."

"Am I that good?" Celeste asked.

"You're that good," Ruthana assured her. "You can make sketches while I'm here and finish the painting later, can't you?"

"Yes. But I will have time, if you're to be here three weeks," Celeste said. "I work very fast."

"I'm afraid you won't have time," Ruthana said. "You're going to be married to Philipe. Don't give me no for an answer. You can be cured of agoraphobia. People are all the time."

Celeste rose from the chair. Now the tears had come. "I never really hated you," she said.

"Thank you for that."

"I must find Philipe."

"He was to call me tonight. You can call him from downstairs."

Ruthana had been faintly conscious of wind that was beginning to rattle palm fronds outside and whistle past the room's windows, but suddenly it was as if Sam Lord's Castle had been dealt a blow by a mailed fist. Rain was slashing at the building. The corridor outside the room was open at both ends, and they heard wind screaming through it. Water began running under the locked door and spraying through the metal hurricane shutters.

Estelle's voice was a hundred 747s running up before takeoff, endless trains with whistles screaming in a tunnel. The room door vibrated like a tuning fork. Ruthana went to the bolted door, but realized just in time that to open it would be madness. The force of this wind would batter Celeste and herself against the room walls or suck them out into the corridor like dry leaves.

"We're trapped here together," she yelled at Celeste.

"I know it."

Window glass shattered, sucked against the shutters, and the room door threatened to break off its hinges. When that first window exploded, air rushed from the room, and Ruthana and Celeste gasped for breath in the partial vacuum. Then water was coming in as if from a firehose turned against the shutters.

Ruthana and Celeste retreated to a far corner, away from the windows, and sat on the floor. The room had become a soaking wet shambles. But Estelle's ultimate terror was the sound!

In her mind Ruthana tried to compare it with something familiar, but found that she couldn't. She covered her ears with her hands, but it was no use.

Another window exploded. Ruthana and Celeste moved closer together for comfort.

"I'm worried about Philipe." Celeste spoke into her ear. "If he's home, he'll be safe, but if he was caught looking for me. . . ." She left that thought unfinished.

Hugh! He wouldn't know where she was.

Where was he? Safe in the wine cellar with the others, or looking for her?

"Philipe's probably safe somewhere," Ruthana reassured Celeste. "It's Hugh Laidman I'm worried about."

The Castle was rocking on its foundation.

CHAPTER 14

Estelle's eye reached Saba just when Ruthana thought she would go screaming mad. It was the stillness of death that hung over the small island.

"Ruthana?" Hugh's voice, and his fist pounding the door. "Are you in there?"

"Coming," she sang out. Ruthana shot the bolt and opened the door. "Celeste Simon is with me."

Hugh's face was haggard. He was bleeding from a small cut over his right eye. "I've been crazy," he said. "Were you here with her all this time?"

"Yes, she was," Celeste answered him. "I must call my cousin."

"There's no way," Hugh said. "Every telephone line on Saba blew away. But your brother is downstairs looking for you."

Celeste rushed past Hugh. He stepped back, surprised. "What gives with her?" he asked Ruthana.

"I'll explain later," Ruthana said. "You've cut your head."

Hugh raised a hand to his forehead, then looked at the blood on his fingers. "So I have. I didn't know."

Hugh stood in the doorway. Ruthana came to him, and with arms around his neck, pressed the full length of her body against his. She drew his face to hers, and it was an unbridled kiss. "I love you, Laidman," she sang. "I love you, Hugh."

Hugh's eyes widened. "So what gives with you?" he asked.

She kissed his cut forehead. "Do you know that you ask too many questions?" She kissed him again on the lips, and this time his arms tightened around her. Hugh moaned. Ruthana showed him no mercy.

They stood apart.

Hugh threw back his head. "Estelle, you bitch, I love *you!*"

"Which reminds me," Ruthana said. "Now she's going to blow in the opposite direction. How is that wine cellar?"

"Crowded."

"Bolt the door, Hugh." Ruthana pointed to the far corner. "We'll sit over there."

Hugh did as he was told.

Estelle's second breath of vengeance wasn't as strong as her first. Her encounter with Saba had been a lesson. Even a goat had defied her. Clarence, from the shelter of the cave he'd shared with that strange woman, stared into the worst she could do with his yellow eyes and didn't flinch.

So Estelle took a last, halfhearted swipe at Saba and went into her death dance over the Gulf of Venezuela. She shrank, her winds died, and she became a mere storm.

* * *

Reverend Hans Baedacker was a frightened
and confused young man. Fresh from divinity
school in Holland, he'd been summoned to Saba
from Saint Martin to perform a marriage in
Windwardside's century-old Dutch Reformed
church. Reverend Hans was afraid of flying. No
one warned him about the airport on Saba.

If that wasn't enough, the American who had
summoned him hadn't posted banns.

Reverend Hans stopped worrying about this
oversight when he learned he was supposed to
marry, also, the administrator of Saba and a
woman everyone said was his twin sister!

To complicate matters further, there was the
American photographer who wanted to marry
a pretty model and had suggested a *triple wedding!*

Reverend Hans Baedacker had yet to perform
his first *single* wedding!

Reverend Hans poured another glass of Dutch
gin that the hotel keeper had so thoughtfully
provided, raised his eyes in the direction of
heaven, and asked for guidance.

A mailboat would come to Saba tomorrow.

No man should be asked to takeoff from that
sliver of an airport, once God had wished him

in. Reverend Hans downed the yellow gin in a gulp.

Six people were going to be married in the morning.

Love—the way you want it!

Candlelight Romances

THE PASSING BELLS

by

PHILLIP ROCK

A story you'll wish would go on forever.

Here is the vivid story of the Grevilles, a titled British family, and their servants—men and women who knew their place, upstairs and down, until England went to war and the whole fabric of British society began to unravel and change.

"Well-written, exciting. Echoes of Hemingway, Graves and *Upstairs, Downstairs.*"—*Library Journal*

"Every twenty-five years or so, we are blessed with a war novel, outstanding in that it depicts not only the history of a time but also its soul."—*West Coast Review of Books.*

"Vivid and enthralling."—*The Philadelphia Inquirer*

A Dell Book $2.75   (16837-6)

Dell Bestsellers

- [ ] **TO LOVE AGAIN** by Danielle Steel $2.50 (18631-5)
- [ ] **SECOND GENERATION** by Howard Fast $2.75 (17892-4)
- [ ] **EVERGREEN** by Belva Plain $2.75 (13294-0)
- [ ] **AMERICAN CAESAR** by William Manchester . . . $3.50 (10413-0)
- [ ] **THERE SHOULD HAVE BEEN CASTLES**
  by Herman Raucher $2.75 (18500-9)
- [ ] **THE FAR ARENA** by Richard Ben Sapir $2.75 (12671-1)
- [ ] **THE SAVIOR** by Marvin Werlin and Mark Werlin . $2.75 (17748-0)
- [ ] **SUMMER'S END** by Danielle Steel $2.50 (18418-5)
- [ ] **SHARKY'S MACHINE** by William Diehl $2.50 (18292-1)
- [ ] **DOWNRIVER** by Peter Collier $2.75 (11830-1)
- [ ] **CRY FOR THE STRANGERS** by John Saul $2.50 (11869-7)
- [ ] **BITTER EDEN** by Sharon Salvato $2.75 (10771-7)
- [ ] **WILD TIMES** by Brian Garfield $2.50 (19457-1)
- [ ] **1407 BROADWAY** by Joel Gross $2.50 (12819-6)
- [ ] **A SPARROW FALLS** by Wilbur Smith $2.75 (17707-3)
- [ ] **FOR LOVE AND HONOR** by Antonia Van-Loon . . $2.50 (12574-X)
- [ ] **COLD IS THE SEA** by Edward L. Beach $2.50 (11045-9)
- [ ] **TROCADERO** by Leslie Waller $2.50 (18613-7)
- [ ] **THE BURNING LAND** by Emma Drummond $2.50 (10274-X)
- [ ] **HOUSE OF GOD** by Samuel Shem, M.D. $2.50 (13371-8)
- [ ] **SMALL TOWN** by Sloan Wilson $2.50 (17474-0)

At your local bookstore or use this handy coupon for ordering:

Dell | **DELL BOOKS**
P.O. BOX 1000, PINEBROOK, N.J. 07058

Please send me the books I have checked above. I am enclosing $_____
(please add 75¢ per copy to cover postage and handling). Send check or money
order—no cash or C.O.D.'s. Please allow up to 8 weeks for shipment.

Mr/Mrs/Miss _____

Address _____

City _____ State/Zip _____

**Sometimes you have to lose
everything before you can begin**

To Love Again
Danielle Steel

Author of *The Promise* and
Summer's End

Isabella and Amadeo lived in an elegant
and beautiful world where they shared their
brightest treasure—their boundless, en-
during love. Suddenly, their enchantment
ended and Amadeo vanished forever. With
all her proud courage could she release the
past to embrace her future? Would she ever
dare TO LOVE AGAIN?

A Dell Book $2.50 (18631-5)